MINI BITES

BY S.M MILES

DON'T JUDGE

It was noisy in the Brunel. People sat at the ground floor café or popped in and out of the many shops. A person could easily get lost amongst the crowds. Sally had not lost her target. He was stood outside a beauty shop; it was clear he was waiting for someone. Sally was sat on one of the benches positioned by both the entrance and exit doors.

Her target was John Smite, 32 years old, recently divorced and a father of one. He was a security guard, off sick due to a work injury. That is where Sally came in. His employers did not believe him, and Sally had been hired to find proof John was faking his injuries.

So far Sally had enough circumstantial evidence but no real, hard proof. Sally was in plain sight of her target but at 5' 2" tall and over 18st in weight, she was easily dismissed as being anybody to look out for. Not a single one of her targets had ever considered the short, fat lady could be following them.

Sally once followed a cheating husband for 2 weeks. She had physically bumped into him 3 times and he had been warned he was being followed – his wife had become drunk and blurted it out – but still he never suspected Sally. The phrase "Never judge a book by its cover" had never been more appropriate.

Sally had been following her recent target for 4 days so far, until today he had only ever driven to the odd shop or visit a friend, this was the first time Sally had a real chance to watch him and get a sense of him. his apparent injuries included: severe back strain, vertigo, and stress. These all related to an apparent fall he suffered while at work. No report had ever been made and his coworkers swear it never happened. The company he worked for had a reputation to uphold and wanted clear proof of any wrongdoing before they dismissed him.

Sally loved her job. She never would have thought taking a simple receptionist job would have led to something like this. Sally often felt like a spy or special agent uncovering the truth and serving justice but without all the red tape rules. Sally sat on the bench, her phone in her hands and pulled the odd face as if she were playing games on her phone. In truth she was recording her target. Nobody paid her any attention. They never did.

A young lady came out of the beauty shop – not the target's ex-wife. Sally had seen pictures of her – she walked up to the target and gave him a passionate kiss. The target lifted the lady up and swung her around, please to see her and by her greeting. They walked off hand in hand. Sally followed.

6 shops later, 8 bags in total – all of which the target carried – and they were finally ready to head back to the carpark. Sally watched and recorded it all. Today had given her all the proof she needed to help her clients. Sally watched the lady's car pull away with the target in and stopped recording.

Sally walked back to the Brunel parking, got in her car, and drove away. Sally drove back to the office and checked her recording had uploaded to her computer successfully. It had. All she had left to do was the paperwork. Another case closed.

All done, Sally had saved her work and was about to lock up when Bobby – a colleague – came running in looking frantic.

'They spotted me Sal. I was on the phone with the Mrs and screwed up.'

Before Sally could respond 3 large men came crashing into the office receptionist area. Since Sally stopped working as the receptionist, they only ever hired a morning temp to cover the basics, which thankfully meant nobody was there who could get harmed. Sally was not 100% sure who the men were but she could take a wild guess and was noticeably confident she would be damn near spot on. Sally put her hands up and stood in front of

Bobby.

'Sorry gentlemen but we are closed for the day. I was about to lock up so would appreciate it if you come back tomorrow with whatever is troubling you,' Sally was ignored, as she had expected would happen. Her words were ignored, as well as her stature.

The first man went to get past Sally but she side stepped to block his way. He tried again; Sally did the same move. He looked down at Sally with a mixture of amusement and disgust in his eyes. Sally had seen the look many times, and always from complete strangers. Disgust at her size, and amusement that she thought they would listen to her. The man faced Sally and placed his left hand on her left shoulder, he gave Sally a shove. Sally was ready for him; his move had left his left side wide open to her. Sally clenched her right fist and punched him in his side. Sally heard him gasp in shock and pain before he bent over, trying to protect his ribs from further assault. The other 2 men stood in shock. They could not comprehend someone who looked like Sally could possibly do what they had just witnessed. Sally was also very used to this reaction and thought again about that old saying, maybe she should get it as a tattoo she mused.

'You going to leave or do one of you think you can do better than your friend?'

They left. They carried their friend out as fast as they could.

They made Sally smile. Them and others like them – almost everyone she had met in over 2 decades – never failed to make her smile. Sally knew how she looked – even if she were blind she would know how she looked – but in this day and age why did people still insist on assuming she must be inadequate in almost everything just because she was fuller than the average plus size lady? Short and fat did not equal useless. Sally took great pleasure in reminding people like them, that quite simple truth.

Bobby was just as shocked as the men had been. He had heard her say she was capable of looking after herself but like so many others, he never believed her. Now he knew better and was so glad he had come running back to the office and found Sally there.

Bobby had not wanted Sally to move up from being a receptionist. He passionately believed that what they did was men's work and was sure Sally would fail spectacularly. Her appearance – size and weight – had also convinced him she would not be up to it. But he was man enough to admit when he was wrong, and he had been very wrong. Sally had proved time and time again she was an asset. So far, she never had a case she had not been able to close. Sally had never been spotted by a target, or anyone close to a target and always covered every angle. On top of that, she had now just saved his arse. He was more pleased than ever he had been outvoted and Sally had been hired.

Sally was woken the next morning when her phone rang. It was mike, the senior investigator.

'I have a new case for you kiddo. Another employee playing sick, I have left the file on your desk. Oh, and Bobby told me about last night. I hope you don't want security wages as well,' Mike hung up laughing. He was a good man and Sally had nothing but support for him, even if his jokes were rather corny.

Sally got dressed and jumped in her car. She loved the excitement of a new case, and employees playing sick where her favourite. Followed closely by cheating spouses, nobody liked being done over whether in love or work. If you are doing someone wrong and Sally was on the case, you would be caught. There was always proof, and Sally would not rest until she found it.

Sally sat at her desk and looked over the file, 3 pages in total. Page one was a photo of the target, it had clearly been enlarged, most likely from a driver's license. The second page was the fact sheet, name and address of target, company details etc. The final page listed places the target had been recently, courtesy of her credit/debit card transactions. People thought this was not possible, but it was and so much more.

Sally sat a few minutes looking over everything, it was always the best place to start. A shop kept coming up on the transactions, every few days the target would buy something from there. On average, the target went there twice a week. Sally looked the shop up online; it was an herbal shop and it was close to the target's home. Sally would start her investigation there.

The target was Shannon Milts, 26 years old, single, and lived alone. Employed as a supervisor at a gambling establishment. She was off for medical reasons; a copy of a doctor's note was provided. It proved nothing; every case Sally had concerning a sick employee involved a sick note. Now a days, you could get a sick note without even seeing a doctor, so it proved nothing as far as Sally was concerned.

Sally sat in her car and looked around. The herbal shop was situated in a shopping centre known locally as The Orbital. At first glance, Sally could not see the shop she was looking for. She got out of her car and wondered around. There was no sign or map to indicate where the shops were located. Sally took a slow stroll around, she blended in with the other pedestrians and as usual, nobody paid her any attention. Sally walked around the shopping centre twice before she found the herbal shop. It was in the same building as a crystal shop. Sally needed to go through the crystal shop, walk to the back before she got to the herbal shop. There was nowhere she could wait inside either of the shops. Sally could go unnoticed but even she would start to cause suspicion if she just stood around in the same shop for hours.

Sally went back out. She could not move her car closer to sit and wait in and there were no immediate benches outside or nearby. It would not be an easy surveillance job. The only place Sally could find that might work was a café a little further back, by the carpark. If the target went past the café then Sally would be able to spot her, but if she went to the shop via another entrance then Sally would miss her. As Sally walked towards the café, she spotted a few more possibilities. A library – she could sit by the window and pretend to read a book while she kept an eye out for her target – and there was a sprinkler close to it filled with children running through the water and laughing as people stood and watched. One place would not do for long surveillance, but she could swap between them and have better luck.

2 days and no sign of the target, Sally had once waited a whole week before she had her first glimpse of her target, so she was not dejected. Her only issue was with the other entrances. So many and not enough places to hide. It was a lovely place to wait though. The café's food and drink was reasonable and cooked her food exactly right. The library was quiet, and she could sit for hours without being disturbed. The fountain was entertaining but not a place she could hang around for long, good parents paid attention to who was watching their children and who was stood around without a child. But it was a good place to walk around to stretch her legs.

It was the 4th day of surveillance when Sally first spotted her target. Sally watched as her target walked around the fountain and headed straight for the shop. Sally was in the library; she left her book on the table and got up. She waited a few beats then followed. The target was in the herbal shop while Sally hung back in the crystal shop, pretending to look for just the right one. Sally could not hear what was being said but she could easily read their body language. The target was relaxed, comfortable with her surroundings and friendly with the lady at the till. The target walked with ease, giving the impression of not a care in the world. Sally would enjoy bringing this fraud down. Healthy people who played at being sick really would Sally up. Sally knew people who had disabilities, either from birth or due to real injuries but they just got on with life, did the best they could and never let self-pity take over. Then there were people like the target, people who just wanted and easy life and to do as little as possible.

The herbal shop had a little section cornered off, there was a chair with a temporary partition – offering semi privacy – the target sat on the chair and a middle-aged lady sat opposite her. There was no way Sally could get any closer and listen in, and she could not hang around in the crystal shop much longer – there was only one other customer – so Sally went back outside and moved in the direction of the fountain so she could wait for the target.

The target came out a few minutes later, she was carrying a

box with a picture of a bee on it. Sally followed the target as far as her car then watched her leave. Sally went back to the herbal shop, found the box the target had – it was a box of honey pills – and paid for it – it would go on her expenses – then headed back to the office.

It was 4 more days before Sally spotted her target again. The target did the same as before, headed straight to the herbal shop. Once again, the target sat in the chair and spoke to the lady. Once again, she came out with a box, headed back to her car, and left. The only difference was the box, it was a box, not honey pills but peppermint tea.

Sally checked out the target's home. There the target stayed indoors for days until she went back to the herbal shop. Sally watched for 2 weeks and nothing changed. The target only left her home when she went to the herbal shop. She had groceries delivered and the only visitor she had was the postman. The target went through a lot of toilet rolls in a week for just one person and always purchased something different at the herbal shop, so far Sally had watched her buy honey pills, peppermint tea, ground flaxseed, fennel tea, camomile tea and ginger supplements.

The target always looked healthy and at ease. There was no sign of pain or distress and Sally was no closer to what the target's apparent medical problem was. It was obvious to Sally that the target was faking, she just wished she could prove it. The target was smart, hiding in her home but she should work on her appearance, it screamed healthy.

3rd week of surveillance and Sally needed a change. She went to the public toilets; she had a plan. Sally had been following the target for weeks now and the shop staff were beginning to recognise her, she only ever purchased what the target purchased so she needed to change things up. Changing her clothes would not be enough, Sally needed to change her look as well. Sally sat in a cubicle and rummaged around in the bag she had with her, she got out a black wig, brown contact lenses – to change her eye colour – and a few fake tattoos, people always remembered tattoos.

A noise came from the cubicle next to hers. The lady in the cubicle was crying. The lady gasped in pain, there was no denying that. That crying could not be faked. Sally was at a loss of what to do. Should she stop changing and help the lady? Should she carrying on changing and leave? She Sally offer help? But what help could she give. Sally could hear the pain through the lady's tears, and it made Sally feel extremely uncomfortable, she felt she was invading the lady's privacy. Sally loved spying on people but for once she felt there was a limit. Sally stood unsure what to do when she heard the entrance door open. Sally heard footsteps then a quick retreat and the entrance door open and close again. That was it, Sally knew she had to do something.

Sally put everything back in her bag and exited her cubicle. Sally knocked on the lady's cubicle door, she did not wait for a reply before offering help.

'Sorry to bother you. I could not help but hear you crying and wondered if there is anything I can do to help? Can I get you something or someone?'

There was a pause, then a faint mumbled no thanks from inside the cubicle. Sally thought about trying again but decided against it, the lady was in enough clear distress as it was, and Sally did not want to increase it. Sally went back to her cubicle, finished getting changed and went outside. Sally realised the time; her target always went to the herbal shop by 10am and it was already 10.15am. Sally would head over to the target's home but for now she wanted to know who the lady in the toilet was. Sally loved uncovering mysteries and she could not just walk away when there was something to solve.

Over the next 10 minutes, several women went into the public toilets and more or less ran back out within seconds. It could not be long now. Sally stood, trying to not make it obvious she was staring at the toilet entrance. The pain she heard in those tears; the deep gut-wrenching sobs could not be faked. Even the best actors could not do it justice, cries like that came from the soul. Sally needed to know who it was.

Her target was a fake, she was always smiling, she showed no visible signs of injuries or medical problems but the toilet lady – how Sally was referring to her – was in true pain. The toilet lady needed help and support not her fake target and it made Sally want to catch her target even more.

The toilet entrance door opened and out came her target. Sally stood gobsmacked and in that moment she realised she had been just like the others and judged a book by the covers and made assumptions.

I KNOW

Jane sat with Stacey in the break room. Stacey was worried and looking for advice. Stacey would be going to her girlfriends after work to meet her family, and once she got there her girlfriend would be coming out to her family. Stacey was worried. Stacey had already come out to her family; she no longer hid her sexuality from anyone. Stacey had to be true to herself and that meant in every way, she did remember the fear though. Fear her family would disown her. Fear she would lose friends and be completely alone. So many fears, but she had to be herself and tell all. Stacey had been lucky, her family and friends – most of them – had accepted her and carried on as normal.

Her girlfriend Molly was the sweetest, kindest person Stacey had ever met and Stacey could talk to her for hours. Stacey had already introduced Molly to her family, now it was Molly's turn. Stacey was not concerned with meeting Molly's family; she was worried with how they might react to Molly coming out. Molly lived with her mum and little sister and spoke highly of them, how they could talk openly about anything and were always there for each other, but it could all change. Stacey had lost some friends and the odd family member herself – she did not care though; it was their loss not hers – and Stacey had ex's whose family's had turned nasty when they found out. She did not want anything like that for Molly, it would break her.

'Sorry to burden you with all this. I just need someone to talk it all through with,' Stacey said to Jane.

'Honestly, it's ok. Molly is lucky to have someone like you

in her corner. You go to hers later and be there for her. I feel very strongly it will all go swimmingly, you must believe. I can see how much you love her; your eyes light up when you mention her. That love will shine through.'

Stacey thanked Jane and stood up, her shift was not finished yet and she needed to get on. She was feeling better though. Jane was easy to talk too; a good listener and Stacey was grateful to work with her.

Jane was not just a co-worker, she had a vested interest in Stacey, a need to find out more about her. It was clear how much Stacey loved Molly, and this pleased Jane, but Jane had only befriended Stacey to find out more about her. The more they talked, the happier Jane became, she was pleased with Stacey.

Jane had a lot to sort out and only a couple of hours to do it in. Shopping first, then tidy up and cook a meal. Jane's eldest had some news to share at tea time and Jane had some news of her own. They both a good spaghetti Bolognese and decided to cook that with all the trimmings. It would be easier if Jane waited and got her eldest to help her, but she had enough on her plate already and Jane did not want to add to her distress.

Tonight would mark the beginning of a new chapter in both of their lives and Jane wanted, no needed it to go perfectly. For both their sakes. Jane put aside her nerves and decided to take her own advice and just believe it would all work out.

The time soon flew by, the meal was cook and keeping warm, Jane laid the table and sat at the kitchen table and waited for her daughter to come home.

Jane heard the key in the lock, she stood up and walked back to the cooker and began to dish up the meal. Molly sheepishly entered the kitchen.

'Mum, I have someone I want you to meet.'

Molly stood and waited. She was terrified everything would go terribly wrong. She was terrified she would get thrown out. Terrified she would get disowned, lose her family. Molly's girlfriend's family had welcomed her with open arms, they had accepted her as part of their family, and it had been a real eye opener.

Molly never even realised she was a lesbian until Stacey came into her life. Stacey was a breath of fresh air, and Molly regretted nothing. They had been friends, then Stacey had made a move. Stacey had leaned forward and kissed Molly. At first, Molly was shocked and ran away, it was the first time that had ever happened. Molly avoided Stacey and kept quiet about what had happened. Stacey respected her decision and left her alone, but the kiss would not go away. It played over and over again in Molly's head; it would not stop replaying in her head. Molly had to see Stacey again, she had to do something about it. Molly met Stacey at hers, and they went upstairs. Stacey remained quiet while Molly did all the talking. Stacey was respectful and let Molly get all her thoughts and feeling out in the open.

The more Molly spoke, the more she realised how much she cared for Stacey. The kiss flashed in her mind again. Molly took the plunge, she leaned forward and kissed Stacey. Stacey responded and the kiss grew more passionate. It went from there. Molly spent the night at Stacey's, with Stacey. It was the happiest and most satisfying night of Molly's life. Molly understood what she had been missing in her life. Molly finally understood why she had always felt out of place, not quite the same as those around her. That realisation was momentous to Molly and she knew there was no going back. She could only move forward with her life and that meant letting people see her true self.

Jane stayed with her back to them, she did not want to give away her surprise just yet. It did not last long; Jane was too excited to keep the suspension going any longer. Jane grabbed the plates and turned to face them.

'Take a seat, food's ready. Stacey, I hope you like spaghetti Bolognese,' Jane smiled at the shocked faces she was greeted with. Jane placed the plates on the table and sat down. Jane faced Molly and Stacey and explained how she had found out about them weeks ago. She had seen them kiss and was shocked. But once that wore off, Jane could admit she had never seen Molly happier. After realising Stacey worked in the same building as herself, Jane had made it her mission to get to know her better. Jane needed to find out what type of person she was and if she genuinely cared about her eldest. Jane was a single parent and very protective of her children, but she had nothing to fear with Stacey. Her love for Molly had always been clear and when she confided in Jane about her coming out to her family, Jane knew she had to make it the best coming out meal in history.

'Every parent just wants the best for their child. Molly has been the happiest she has ever been, and that is thanks to you Stacey. The only thing left to say is welcome to the family and eat up.'

SLEEP ON IT

Evie was feeling the pressure. She loved David with all her heart but was it right for them to run away. Could they really be happy without the support of their families? They were still young, only early 20's, maybe they were rushing into things. Their families were dead set against them being together, maybe they were right. Evie had been taught to respect her elders and that parents knew best. If they thought David was not good enough for her, maybe they were right. Evie's love for David could be just a phase, as her dad said. Maybe she would get over him and find someone who made her as happy, or happier. Maybe it was just young love, as her mum said.

Or maybe it was true love and David was her soulmate. Could she risk pushing David away and losing him forever. Could she risk giving up her only chance of real happiness just to please her parents? There was no one to talk too, nobody she could confide in. David would be heartbroken if he knew she had doubts, and she already knew how her parents felt about things. They were willing to disown her if she continued her relationship with David. Evie had to choose between losing her parents and keeping the possible love of her life or stay with David and lose her parents forever. Either way, Evie would lose someone.

Evie laid down to sleep. It was going to be along; fretful night and Evie was not looking forward to it but there was nothing she could do. She would just have to sleep on it and hope it was clearer in the morning.

Evie stood in shock; the building was in crumbles. Dust had

not yet settled. Screams were deafening. Evie could not move; she was stuck to the spot. Feelings came rushing to her, memories emerged from deep within. Evie was in London, 1942. Bricks and debris covered the ground. The rubble had once been her fiancé's place of work. Now it was gone. Smoke and dust filled the air. People ran around screaming, whiles others were on their knees crying. Sirens sounded and men in uniforms ushered people away from the damage and the danger.

Evie was there to meet her fiancé for lunch. She had arrived just as the building crumbled to the ground. Evie was moved back. She was pushed further away by men in uniform. Her legs still did not work, she was numb. She could not talk, scream, or even move by herself. Shock had taken complete control over her. Evie could hear talking to hear, but she could not understand the words. She could see fuzzy faces in front of her but was unable to respond. She was in a daze.

Her fiancé's face flashed in her mind. He looked different and had a different name, but Evie knew it was David. She could sense it was him. Her heart broke with the knowledge he was gone. Evie heard his name get mentioned as one of the missing possibly deceased, and that is when she screamed. The scream came out of nowhere and took all by surprise, but Evie could not stop screaming. She screamed of loss, of pain and of anguish. She screamed loud with no end in sight. Evie felt a little scratch on her arm, and everything began to fade.

People clapped and cheered. Evie was in a crowd. Evie was deeply enjoying herself; she was at a theatre with hundreds of others. The Royal Court Theatre was the best theatre there was, and Evie was there. Her husband was in the play. It was 1893. They were watching *The Amazons*, and Evie was loving it. Her husband had a major role and it was his big break. Evie knew he would be brilliant. He was incredibly talented. Her heart filled with pride and joy when he walked on stage. He looked into the crowd, searching for her. His smile filled the room when he found her, his smile was for her alone.

Evie found the play very amusing, she laughed and clapped with the others. At the end of the play, there was a standing ovation. Evie went to the back to wait for her husband. When he came out, people rushed at him, he had been superb. He smiled and said a few words, all the while moving his way through the crowd to get to Evie. She was all he wanted, the only reason he had to be there.

It was when he was finally at her side that Evie recognised him. he looked and sounded different but, it was David. Evie could sense it.

Evie ran across an open field. Wind gently blowing through her hair. Evie ran in the sun. she ran for pure joy. For the joy of being free and in the open air. Life was hard, they did not have much. Barely enough to scrap by, but they were free. The farm was in ruins and pigs had been stolen. A fox, or another animal had attacked the chickens not long ago and now they had trouble laying eggs. Their home was falling apart, and the future looked bleak, but they had each other. They had sunshine. They had love for each other. They had a wonderful daughter they both adored and their freedom. No matter what life threw at them, Evie knew she would always have her David. She smiled as she neared their crumbling home and saw him playing in the garden with their daughter. Both laughing it made her laugh.

Evie woke up. It was morning. The dream was still fresh in her mind. Each time it had been David. Different lives. Different places. Different person, but still always David. He was her soulmate, the love of her life. He was who she was meant to be with and who she should chose. Evie no longer had any doubts about their love. It was destined.

LOVE NOTES

Sharon looked at the note. She had found it on the floor, by the front door, inside her flat. Someone must have slid it under her front door while she had been out, she had only popped to the shops. It was typed, not hand written. It was on A4 paper, 1 sentence, 3 words in the centre of the page. *I LOVE YOU*.

There was no name on it, so it could be meant for someone else. Someone who would know who the sender was. Someone who would appreciate it and not be a tad freaked out like Sharon was. She had only moved in 2 months ago, from another town and knew nobody before she moved. There was no envelope which meant the note had been delivered by the person who wrote it. It could be meant for the previous tenant. That made sense, Sharon relaxed once more.

Sharon put the note on the kitchen table and left it. Her neighbour Rachel was bound to know the previous tenant and Sharon could ask her, find out if it was worth trying to send the note on to the rightful recipient.

With the worry now gone, Sharon went back to work. She had a deadline to beat and needed to get a move on. Sharon lost track of time, when she finally took a break and looked up it was gone 9pm. Too late to speak to Rachel about the note. She would do it tomorrow.

When Sharon got home the next day from visiting her parents, she was greeted with another note. Same paper. Same type font and size. Folded the same way and delivered the same way. The only difference was the words. This note read: *YOU ARE*

BEAUTIFUL.

If it was delivered by the person who wrote it, then Sharon guessed it was most likely for the previous tenant. If it was delivered by someone else, then Sharon guessed it was delivered to the wrong flat. Simple mistakes.

Sharon picked up the previous note from the kitchen table and went next door to Rachel's. Sharon felt a little silly but knocked anyway. Rachel answered on the first knock, she opened the door wide and let Sharon in. They went to the living room and Sharon handed Rachel the notes. As Rachel looked them over, Sharon explained.

'I don't know what to say. The previous tenants were an elderly couple. They moved out over a year ago. The flat remained empty until you moved in, it was given a deep clean and a fix up but that was it, nobody else lived there.'

It was not what Sharon had wanted or expected to hear. They could not be for her, nobody knew her. She moved from another town and knew nobody here before she moved. She had only been in the town for 3 months, 1 month at a B&B before she got the flat. She worked from home and apart from the polite head nod and murmured hello to some people she saw in passing, Rachel was the only person she actually spoke too. It had to a case of wrong address, there was no other explanation for them.

Sharon was greeted to another note the next day. Same as before but with different words again. This note read: **THESE ARE FOR YOU SHARON.**

Rachel! It had to be her; she was the only person Sharon had spoken to about the notes. Who else would know to put that? Well, it was not funny, and Sharon would make sure Rachel stopped.

Sharon stomped across to Rachel's and banged on her door. Rachel answered and Sharon pushed her way in, without giving Rachel a chance to stop her.

'What is wrong with you? I came to you for help and it was you all along.'

'What was me? What are you on about?' Rachel was confused.

Sharon showed Rachel the latest note.

'I didn't write the notes. I do not love you; I would not do anything to jeopardise our friendship. I swear it's not me.'

'Who else would it be? Who else would know I doubted they were for me then poof, I am told they are for me. That is more than just a coincidence do not you think. Just admit it!' Sharon was beginning to lose her temper.

'I swear it wasn't me. I don't know who is writing them, or why, but it's not me!' Rachel did not know what else she could say. She was as shocked and confused as Sharon.

Sharon walked away. There was no point in continuing to argue with Rachel and Sharon would end up hitting her if Rachel did not admit it, so best if she just leave. Sharon crumpled the notes up and threw them in her kitchen bin. It was over.

It was not over.

There was another note waiting for Sharon the next day. This note read: ***I LOVE YOUR WORK***.

What the hell? Sharon never told anyone what she did for a living. Only her boss knew her real name in her professional world. Not even Rachel knew what she did, only that she worked from home. What was going on? Sharon crumpled up the note and threw it away with the others.

Sharon wanted to catch the person – likely Rachel – in the act. She made sure she stayed in the next day. Sharon positioned a chair facing her front door and waited. And waited. And waited. No note came.

It was 4 days before Sharon received another note. It read: ***I HAVE MISSED YOU.***

Again, Sharon instantly thought of Rachel. Who else would miss her? Sharon was an only child and saw or spoke to her parents daily, besides, they would not do something like this. the only other person Sharon had contact with was Rachel.

Sharon decided to leave her own note for Rachel. In no uncertain terms, she explained she would get the police involved if

Rachel did not stop immediately.

The notes did not stop.

The next note came the very next day and read: ***DON'T IGNORE ME!***

Sharon had had enough. She kept her promise and got the police involved; they took Rachel in for questioning.

It was not Rachel. Sharon got another note while Rachel was still helping the police with their enquiries. The note read; ***TALK TO ME!***

Who was she meant to talk to? Who was behind it? Sharon felt more lost than ever before. She owed Rachel an apology but other than that, Sharon was no clearer on what was happening, or why.

Then the man appeared. It was late in the afternoon when Sharon saw him for the first time. He stood on the path, in the carpark looking up at her flat. He wore a black cowboy hat and long black coat. Sharon was on the 6th floor; the hat hid his features so Sharon could not get a clear look of him. He stood there for hours, just looking up. He said nothing. Made no gestures. Sharon hid behind her curtains and peeked out at him. He left before midnight. Sharon was too frightened to sleep.

He came again the next day, evening time. He stood in the same spot as the day before. Sharon tried to involve the police, but they were not interested. The notes proved useless and it was not illegal for him to stand in a carpark. He said threatening and made no threatening gestures. He was not breaking any laws. Sharon could do nothing.

Sharon had enough. She had no idea what was happening, or why but she was not playing his game anymore. Sharon closed her curtains; made sure her door and windows were locked tight and tried her best to ignore he was out there.

For a week it was the same. The man got there late afternoon/early evening and stood in the same spot. Same hat and coat, same silence. Sharon had the occasional peek, just to see if he was still there but that was it.

Sharon apologised to Rachel, and thankfully, Rachel understood. Rachel admitted she would have thought the same if the roles had been reversed. At least something was going right for Sharon.

The notes continued. They got more threatening. Demanded response. Warned of more to come. The police took the notes but did little else. Sharon was no closer to the end. It was time to do something and stop burying her head in the sand. Sharon purchased a camera. Sharon placed the camera above her front door, it had a clear view of the lift and the stairs. It could see everyone coming and going on her floor.

Everything stopped. The camera caught the postman, her neighbours, their visitors and one other person. A man posting leaflets had come onto her floor, walked to her door, and saw the camera. Sharon thought he looked disappointed, but she could not be sure, he posted a leaflet through her door and did the same to the other flats then left.

For the next week, everything stopped. No more notes. No more man stood outside. Sharon began to relax. It was over, the camera had worked.

Then the camera got broke. Sharon saw who she thought was the same leaflet man walk up to her door and then he went out of view, the camera stopped working a second later. It recorded nothing else and shockingly, there was no note.

The note came the next day. It warned against further actions like that.

Sharon ran to Rachel's and broke down. She needed someone to talk to, someone who understood. Rachel was sympathetic and wanted to be there for her friend, but she was as clueless as Sharon. Neither of them knew who was behind it, or why. Rachel wished she could offer words of wisdom, or a way out of it, but she couldn't see a way out. The only thing she could do was try to make Sharon feel better. Sharon stayed at Rachel's for hours, they talked, they drank and when Sharon left she felt slightly better. Rachel was a real friend and Sharon was glad they had made up.

Sharon wished she had stayed at Rachel's. Sharon did not notice the scratch marks on her door lock when she returned home. Sharon went in, left the lights off, closed and locked her door then went right to bed. As she lay on her bed, staring to drift off, she heard a scraping sound coming from the living room. Sharon sat up in the bed and listened. There it was again. Sharon thought she might have accidently left a window open, she went into the living room and found the light switch.

A knife greeted her. It was dug into the living room table. Sharon stood frozen. She was too scared to move, too scared to look around. The knife glistened in the light. A rustling noise from behind her made Sharon shake. She felt a hand on her shoulder, a firm grip. The hand pushed down. Sharon felt a kick to the back of her right knee and went down. Sharon was on her knees when she felt the hand on her should move to cover her mouth. Then she heard a voice.

'You thought you could just ignore me, after all I did for you. You need to learn some manners,' the voice was male, harsh and low, and full of menace. Sharon did not recognise it. She smelled whisky and cigar smoke. She could almost taste the stale smoke on her fingers. Sharon tried to talk but could not. she was forced to the ground. Face down. Her assailant sat on her back. Sharon could not move, but she could talk now.

'Please, I don't know what you think I have done.'

There was no response. No answer. No demand to shut up. He just remained on her back and stayed silent. Sharon wanted to say more, to beg but she did not know if it would aggravate him more or not. She began to cry, from fear and frustration.

He broke the silence.

'Talk some more. Say something else.'

It was an odd request, but Sharon did as she was told.

There was silence, then a faint *fuck!*, then silence again. A minute later, the man stood up. Sharon was told to stay still and not look at him. She did as she was told. Sharon heard him say fuck a few more times, then heard her front door open, then slam shut. Sharon could hear running. Sharon heard the stairs door bang shut, the sound echoed. Sharon remained on the ground, she wanted to be sure he was gone.

Sharon waited. Sharon listened. There was no other sounds, only the tick tock of her kitchen clock could be heard. Sharon slowly stood up. She shakily made her way to her sofa and collapsed on it. Why had he suddenly left? He could have done anything to her, but he just left. Sharon was happy he was gone but was more confused than ever. Did his sudden departure mean he would be back again? She did not know. She was scared.

There was a sudden banging on her door and Sharon realised she had been screaming.

'Sharon are you ok? It's Rachel, please open the door.'

In a daze, Sharon managed to stand up, walk to the door and open it. As soon as she saw Rachel, Sharon fainted. Rachel saw the knife dug in the table. Rachel carried Sharon to the sofa and rang the police, she demanded someone come out right away. Before they arrived, Sharon woke and – brokenly – explained what had happened.

After the police left, Sharon went with Rachel to hers. She could not sleep in her own flat, she did not know if she would ever be able to sleep there again.

1 week later, Rachel came home with news.

'You're safe now, it really is over.'

Rachel handed Sharon the newspaper shew as holding. There was a picture of her attacker. A woman called Sharon had been brutally murdered. She lived in a block of flats with a remarkably familiar sounding name to her own.

Wrong address all along.

NOT AGAIN

Mandy had gone quiet. June knew something was wrong. Mandy was sat on the sofa, with her feet up and her tablet in her hands. June snuck up behind and looked at the tablet. It was open on Mandy's email account. June could read the message Mandy was looking at. It was from her ex, Jaime. She missed Mandy, she was sorry for lying to her, for cheating on her, Mandy was the best thing to ever happen to her, blah, blah, blah.

June was livid. That total waste of space was trying to worm her way back in to Mandy's life again. She had already hurt, used, and disrespected Mandy so many times, June had lost count. Jaime was Mandy's first love, and she used that to her advantage every chance she got.

The last time Mandy had given Jaime another chance, she had been perfect for 2 whole months. Jaime had done everything right. She had laid on the charm, said all the right things, Mandy had soon been hooked again. It didn't last long. Once it was clear Mandy was besotted with her again, Jaime played her mind games once more. Just like every other time. Small comments about other women's appearance. Comments about how Mandy was dressed. Little remarks about Mandy's weight or lifestyle, things she did or didn't enjoy doing. Jaime accused Mandy of being boring for not wanting to go clubbing all the time. Mandy preferred snuggling up and watching a film, which Jaime knew

Then other things came up which hadn't been a problem when she had been sweet talking Mandy. The distance between was used as an excuse to not see each other. No matter what

Mandy suggested, it was dismissed. Jaime was too busy working to talk, she couldn't even manage a quick text on her breaks. Jaime was too tired to visit but could play pool with her friends or travel miles to meet up with friends.

On the very rare occasions Jaime would visit, she would have an excuse ready to leave as soon as she got what she had come for. That was all Jaime wanted from Mandy, to feel good. Mandy was just there to make Jaime feel good and wait for her.

It all took its toll on Mandy. She was made to feel unworthy, unloved, and unwanted. It chipped away at Mandy. She was too fat, so went on one extreme diet after another in the hopes of pleasing Jaime. It didn't work. Mandy would try to do more, be more, but it made no difference. Jaime still played her games and used Mandy for her own needs only.

If Mandy tried talking to Jaime about it, say how she felt, Jaime accused her of nagging and doing her head in. If Mandy didn't do what Jaime wanted, when she wanted it then she was accused of not loving her and Jaime might as well find someone else. Mandy would keep quiet and hope against all odds that it would be different this time, that Jaime meant what she said for once. It never worked out that way. Mandy always ended up hurt. Jaime always left, and Mandy got hurt more.

June had seen the fallout Mandy times. She had witnessed first-hand, the impact Jaime had on Mandy. They first met over 5 years ago. Every time Mandy started to move on from Jaime, really get on with her life, Jaime would come creeping back. Tell Mandy what she wanted to hear, longed to hear. Mandy would give Jaime another chance, she yearned for it to work out, for it to be real. It never was. It never lasted.

Mandy would never be enough for Jaime. Mandy would never have the Jaime she longed for. Jaime was a manipulative cow who only thought of her own wants and needs. Mandy deserved better, and if June could physically block Jaime from ever going near Mandy again, she would in a heartbeat.

Mandy was amazing, kind, sweet, loving and if June swung that way she would have snapped Mandy up years ago. Mandy was her best friend and deserved to be loved, to be wanted and to be treated properly. June would do anything to keep Jaime away from her. To stop Mandy from being hurt.

June stood up from where she was crouched behind the sofa.

'Don't give her any more chances. If you want to hate me, you can, but I will not let her hurt you again.'

June took Mandy's tablet and replied Jaime, telling her what for, and then blocked her. Mandy's phone beeped. It was Jaime. June blocked her number.

'Come on, let's go out. No need to hang around here thinking about a no good, waste of space like her,' June said as she grabbed their coats.

Mandy put her coat on. She was lucky to have June in her life. She had lost so many friends over the years thanks to her love for Jaime – they got fed up of convincing her how much better she would be without Jaime – but June had stayed. June had stuck by her. June had her back and would always look out for her.

Who needed a heartbreaker when you had a best friend like June. Mandy smiled for the first time since she saw the email. She was done with Jaime, this time for good. June would keep her strong.

I WAS WRONG

There he is again. I am not imagining this. Three days now this guy has been following me, and not discreetly either. He wants me to know he's watching that he will always be there watching me, following me and I have absolutely no idea why.

The first time I saw him, I was on my way home from work. Saturday, shortly after 11pm, I saw him as I passed by the kebab shop. He was stood outside, slouched against the shop window. I didn't think anything about it, just another person enjoying a weekend out. I still wasn't worried when he came away from the shop and began to walk behind me. I was walking through the town centre and although most places where closed, there were still many clubs, pubs and take away shops still open. I assumed he was just moving along to one of those, maybe meeting up with some friends or he changed his mind about a kebab and fancied something else to eat instead.

Either way, I wasn't worried. I got more suspicious the next day when I saw him stood on the corner of my street. He was stood – slouched again – against the wall of the end house. At first, he was looking around as if searching for someone or something. Once he saw me, he stopped looking around. He stared at me. He kept staring as I walked past him, and I could feel him staring at my back as he once again began to follow me.

It didn't matter where I went, work, home, visit a few friends or meals out etc. Or how I got there, by car, by bus or walking, he was always there. I began to wonder if he had been following me for longer than I realised. He always seemed to know where I was going and when I would be there. I had even tried to be unpredictable a few times in the last few days and managed to lose him, but he would always show up. He would be there, watching me, staring at me.

I could not tell you who he is. I could not tell you why he is following me. I really have no idea. I never spoke to him or saw him before all this. I cannot think of anytime or anyway I could have upset him. I really have no idea why he is following me.

I have become accustomed to hate, to stares and vile comments. I have had things thrown at me, been spat at, and been chased a few times. I have been threatened, attacked both verbally and physically. I have been disowned by some family and many friends. I have lived in fear, lived a life of pretence. I have hated myself for years because of who I truly am, and for the way I am treated.

I have had people from all different types of backgrounds, ages, sex, sizes, colours, sexualities – you get the idea – they all felt it perfectly acceptable to treat me like shit. Disregard me as a person and think I got what I deserved when I have been attacked. That I only have myself to blame.

My crime? The horrible, destructive crime I must have committed? Be me. Just finally accept who I am and live my life as the real me.

I was born a male, but it was a mistake. Since a child, I knew something was wrong, but it wasn't until I hit puberty that it began to really make sense. All the pieces fell into place and I finally understood what was wrong.

I did nothing. I was too afraid. The world was not as accepting, not as open as it is now. Sadly, there are people – and always will be – who still refuse to accept and take great pleasure in telling me how disgusting and depraved I am. It was even worse when I was a child. Homosexuality had only become legal a few years before I was born, and as you can imagine, not everyone was happy about it.

My father was a drunk, my mother a cheat, but both believed they knew best. They told us – everyday – how they would feel no regret or remorse in killing us if we brought shame to their home by doing such depraved acts.

As you can imagine, I hid my true feelings. I hid the real me, and it became a way of life. I was scared. Terrified actually. I once saw a gang of lads viciously attack 2 young men just for holding hands.

I tried living as a traditional, respectable heterosexual male. The way I was told I should live and behave. I'm not gay, so it wasn't hard getting girlfriends, or being with them romantically.

The hard part was hiding the real me from them. I was very successful at it, for years I got away with it, then I got caught. My girlfriend at the time came home early from work and caught me wearing her clothes and make up. I had always been so careful, but her early return had been very unexpected. I am sure you can already guess it did not go well. She threw things at me. She chased me around our home with a knife. I hid in the bathroom and changed into the few clothes that were drying on the radiator. She told any and every one she could about it.

I received threat messages and knew my life was in danger. My own father came at me. Attacked me. Called me all manner of disgusting names. Thankfully, he was too drunk to do any damage.

I moved away, changed my name, and hid myself again.

I started therapy. It took years, but I finally opened up and with more years of support, I finally began to live my life as he real me. I will not lie, or sugar coat it, it has been a real struggle. Many times I have questioned if I truly need to be the real me or not. Would it not be easier, safer to just pretend? To carry on as I was before and learn to accept there is a part of me that must remain hidden? Of course, the answer is no. There is no point in living if it is a lie. How can I expect others to accept and love me if I can't accept or love myself.

When I first started living as my true self – dressing and living like the woman I am – it was hard, and I was full of fear. The fear is still there, but I have also grown in courage over the years. I am no longer full of shame. I am no longer willing to hid away to make others feel better. If somebody has a problem with who I am, that is their issue, not mine. I do not do anything to cause trouble though. I keep myself to myself and only visit people and places I know I will be safe and accepted.

Yet now, I am being followed. Being made to feel like a target and I do not like it.

When I see him next, I am prepared. I keep a Stanley knife in my pocket and wrap my fingers around it. I haven't done anything wrong, whatever he truly intends to do to me, he will get a shock. I am done. I will not be intimidated anymore. I will not let others dictate to me how I can dress, who I can be or how I can look. No more will being made to feel there is something wrong with me. No longer a victim and not standing up for myself.

I lead him into a trap. There is a nearby open field and I walk towards it. He follows. If he has friends close by, I will be able to clearly see them approaching. I walk across the field. We are roughly halfway across the field when I stop, I turn around and face him. he stops, unsure what to do.

'Why are you following me?' I ask with more calm in my voice than I feel. I can see him properly now he is up close. He is young, a teenager or young adult perhaps. He is debating what to do, I can see him at a loss of what to do next.

He opens his mouth, then closes it. He opens it once more and utters one word.

'Dad?'

Did I hear him right? Did he really just call me dad? I don't have any children.

'You have me confused with somebody else. I am nobodies dad.' I am beginning to feel sorry for him. He looks hurt. He is not giving up that easily though.

'You are John Milky? Born in Swindon, 1971. Parents Julie and Dave. Older brothers James and Dean. Younger sister Daisy.?'

'How do you know this?'

'Mum told me. She is very sorry how she reacted when she caught you wearing her clothes. She had discovered she was pregnant with me, which is why she had gone home early. She wanted to surprise you, only you surprised her. I want to be clear, mum has never bad mouth you, never tried to make me hate you or anything like that. She was shocked, confused, and full of hormones and fear. She was scared how others would react and of me being taken away from her if you stayed in our lives. She regrets it now but I'm sure you can understand it was a different time and I won't let you or anyone say bad about her. I am not justifying what happened, or how you was treated, but she's my mum and she was only trying to protect me the best way she knew how.' He took a breath and visibly relaxed.

It is a lot to take in. After all these years. I never knew.

I have a son.

I have a son!

ARRIVALS

Sandie sat in traffic. She couldn't see what the holdup was and didn't much care. she had other things on her mind. Julian had proposed before he left. He was back today – Sandie was on her way to the airport to pick him up – and he would want an answer.

Sandie didn't have an answer. She loved Julian but getting married was not on her to do list. Sandie had never been the girl who dreamed about finding Mr Right and getting married. Sandie never made scrapbooks full of wedding themes. She had never looked at a bridal magazine in her life. Sandie didn't have any objections with anybody else who wished to get married. If they were happy, then good for them and she wished them all the best. It just wasn't for her.

Horns beeped at once, from all sides. People got more and more impatient. Sandie put on the C.D player on and turned it up high. She needed to think, to make a decision. She couldn't pick Julian up without an answer for him. He had been so patient, so understanding, he deserved an answer.

Sandie supposed she could get married. At the end of the day, it's only a piece of paper, a ring and possible last name change, everything else stays the same. She could have a simple do. A registry office wedding, no thrills, just sign the paperwork and have a few pictures taken, then back to normal.

Things have changed, she didn't have to obey his every whim anymore. She could still work, still be herself. Women were no longer considered a man's property anymore, she could always get a divorce if it all went pear shaped. When she thought more about it, the only real difference would be how she referred to Julian. He would her husband instead of her boyfriend and she could handle that. She could keep her last name – men can take the woman's last name nowadays if they want – she would get an extra ring, and who doesn't like extra jewellery? It might be doable after all.

Sandie moved forward a few inches, then stopped, breaking hard. She opened her window and stuck her head out. Sandie still couldn't see what the holdup was, but she could now see the airport turnoff sign. At this rate Sandie could probably walk there faster, and she almost considered it, but she still had time left before she would be late so sat and waited. The plane was due to land in 25 minutes, then Julian would need to deboard, get his suitcase and go through customs before he could get to arrivals. Sandie still had time to spare.

Sandie still didn't feel comfortable saying yes. She was more open to the idea of marriage but that was it. Julian had been so romantic when he proposed. He got her father's permission – she found out later – and did the whole down on one knee thing. The ring he chose was perfect in every way. The night he proposed had been very romantic, rose petals from the front door to the dining room where her favourite meal was waiting for her. He had a speech ready, it was so sweet Sandie had cried. He never asked for an answer, in fact he said he would wait until he came back from his trip. He knew how Sandie felt about marriage and he never pressured her, it just made Sandie love him more. They spent the weekend together not once mentioning the proposal, it had been wonderful.

Sandie moved forward again, then break. The horns started up again around her. Sandie checked the time, Julian's plane would have landed by now. She could see the turnoff, it was jammed full of cars. Julian would wait, he knew she was coming, but what if she was stuck in traffic for longer? What if she was there for a few more hours? Julian would think she had dumped him, she didn't want that. She loved him and was leaning more towards yes.

Sandie joined the others and beeped her horn. For once it worked. Slowly but surely, the traffic inched forward. Forward, break. Few more inches, then break again. Forward, break. Sandie could see the bend onto the turnoff. Forward a bit more, break. Forward, slow, forward, break. Sandie was finally on the turnoff. Bit by bit, a few inches at a time Sandie got closer to her destination. Crawl a few more inches, then break. Forward, break. Sandie could see the airport. Forward, break. Forward, break. She was almost there. She would be ready, waiting for Julian. It was gridlock again, nobody was giving way. Sandie could see the airport road, she was so close.

Julian would be off the plane by now, he only had a medium suitcase which wouldn't take him long to get. A few more inches forward, then break. Sandie could see the airport, it was jam-packed. The radio interrupted her C.D.

"I repeat, flight AB123 has been cancelled. The flight was scheduled to land at Bristol airport at 2:15pm but reports came in of a crash, 1 mile from the airport. Reasons unknown."

That was Julian's flight, he was on that plane! Sandie needed to get inside the airport, she needed to know what was going on, they had to know something. The traffic hadn't moved in a while. Sandie wasn't waiting anymore, she had to get there. Sandie moved forward and to her right, she spun the wheel to her left and backed up before the car behind her could close the gap. Sandie spun the wheel to the right and moved forward. Forward and right, back, and left, then forward and right again until she was out of the queue. Cars came at her as they tried to exit the airport, but Sandie didn't care, she pushed her way through, making them move onto the curb.

Why had she been so scared to say yes? Why had she made him wait, put him off for so long? No the time had come, now she was here, Sandie regretted every time she had pushed the idea of marriage to Julian away. Sandie loved him, wanted to spend her life with him. her answer was yes, would always be yes.

Somehow Sandie managed to push her way to the carpark. She edged her way to the entrance without crashing. A taxi was coming out of the taxi rank, Sandie rammed her foot on the accelerator and pushed her way in before the next taxi could move forward. Sandie wasn't the only one with that idea. Sandie jolted forward, her head banged against the dashboard, then her body slammed back. Everything went blank as Sandie passed out.

Sandie didn't know how long she was out cold for, but when she came too, she knew what she had to do. Sandie jumped out of the car – leaving it running – and ran into the airport. Sandie looked for something, anything that would tell her what she needed to know. There was a man with a megaphone, he was surrounded by shouting people. Sandie pushed her way through the crowd. Sandie began shouting along with everyone else. They all wanted to know the same thing, what was going on. The man with the megaphone just kept repeating that the plane had crashed, and they had no further information at this time.

There had to be someone who knew what was happening. Sandie looked around, there were people coming out from the arrivals. Sandie was sure she had seen Julian. Sandie ran over to where she had seen him, he was gone. Maybe she had imagined it. Maybe it was wishful thinking. Or maybe, just maybe he had taken a different flight and was ok. Maybe he hadn't seen her or heard her shouting with all the noise and had gone somewhere else to wait. Sandie looked around, he had to be somewhere. Sandie was sure she saw him again, he was headed to the men's toilet. Sandie ran over, but he was gone again.

Sandie needed a minute, she collapsed to the ground, pushed herself up against the wall and started crying. What was happening? Was it him, or was she going crazy?

Sandie cried louder. Men walked in and out of the toilets, but nobody paid her any attention. Everyone ignored her. They acted as if she wasn't there, which suited Sandie just fine. She didn't want this day to be happening.

A drunk man came out of the toilets, stumbling in her direction. Sandie shouted at him to watch where he was going but he was too drunk to hear. He lost his balance and fell. Sandie braced herself for the impact but there was none. Maybe she had it wrong, maybe he hadn't been as close as she thought. Sandie opened her eyes, she hadn't been wrong about how close he was. The drunk man was on the floor. He landed right on her, or more accurately, right through her!

Suddenly it all made sense. She wasn't being ignored, nobody could see her. She was dead. Sandie thought the crash had been a little bump but now it all came flashing back. When her body went forward, she slammed her head and then back again, her neck had snapped instantly. She was dead.

'You're ready now.'

Sandie looked up. It was Julian.

'Yes. My answer is yes!'

Julian held his hand out. Sandie stood up and took his hand. No matter what came next, they were together.

MEET CHANCE

Why did she have to bump into him? All the people who live in the town – and she was only visiting – why him? Tony was the last person Jody wanted to see. Ever. She had endured his lies, constant cheating, and mental abuse for two years. Then she was free. 5 months, 1 week, 6 days and counting.

They first met in a nightclub. It was Jody's 22nd birthday and she was out with a group of friends. All girls, all dressed like playboy bunnies. They were a crazy bunch, and always up for a laugh and good time.

Tony had also been at the nightclub with a group of his friends. They spent most of the first part of their evening watching Jody and her friends. Jody and her friends noticed – it was hard not too – and danced saucily with each other, teasing Tony, and his friends. Tony soon made a beeline for Jody, his friends quickly followed and before long the 2 groups merged. They laughed. They danced. Jody had the best night of her life – greatest birthday ever. Jody thought it would end there, but she was wrong.

Tony found out where Jody worked. He showed up the next day and refused to leave until Jody agreed to go on a date with him. Jody thought it was very romantic.

Their first date was amazing. Tony was a real gentleman. He opened the doors for her and pulled out her chair. Brought her roses, gave her endless compliments. He asked her questions about her life, likes and hobbies, and really listened to her answers. Above all, he never once tried anything sexual. In fact, if it weren't for him always glancing at her breasts and the hunger in his eyes, Jody would have thought he wasn't interested in her.

It was on their 5th date that Tony made his move. They had just come out of the cinema when Tony pulled Jody close to him, trapping her against the wall and his body and kissed her passionately. Jody wanted more there and then but, Tony ever the gentleman, moved away. On the way home, Jody couldn't stop thinking about their kiss and she wanted more. When they reached her place she invited Tony in, and he eagerly accepted.

They made love. Tony was passionate, gentle, and made sure Jody was satisfied before he took care of his needs. To say it was amazing, would be an understatement.

They became inseparable after that night. They saw each other every day and Tony slept over almost every night. In just a few short months, Jody asked Tony to move in with her. Her family – and most of her friends – were against the idea, they said it was too soon, but Jody wouldn't listen. They said it was still the honeymoon phase and Jody should wait a bit longer, but Jody was in love and wanted to live with Tony. Jody was polite but ignored their concerns.

Jody wished she had listened. Tony changed once he was settled in. tony quit his job within days of moving in and spent his time lounging around, playing games, and complaining when Jody went to work. Tony went from a caring and helpful boyfriend, to a lazy self-centred slob. The only thing that remained the same was their amazing love making.

Then Tony began to pressure Jody to quit her job.

'I miss you when you're at work. Why don't you want to spend your time with me? Don't you love me?' Tony would then cry.

Every time Jody left for work – and when she got home from work – was the same, with maybe a slight variation on the words. And every time Jody got a little closer to quitting her job. She hated seeing Tony so upset.

Jody was on the verge of handing in her notice at work when she got an unexpected promotion. She was thrilled and it strengthened her resolve to stay at work. Jody told Tony all about it when she got home that night, he wasn't happy. Jody explained the promotion meant more money and more extra free time, which meant more time they could spend together.

Tony still wasn't happy. From then on, he would sulk when she left for work, and give her cold shoulder when she got home. Jody was hurting, she didn't want to upset Tony. She loved him, but she also loved her job and hoped it was just an adjustment phase he was going through.

It wasn't. When Jody kept going to work, Tony swapped tactics. Tony accused Jody of cheating on him. All Jody did was work and stay home, when did she have the time to cheat. Jody stopped seeing her friends and family, Tony didn't like it. Jody no longer had any communication with any male friends, it upset Tony. Jody changed her wardrobe to plainer, drabber clothes to please Tony.

'I don't do anything or go anywhere except to work. Then I come home to you because I love you. Please, stop this darling.'

'Stop cheating on me then! I bet you didn't even get a promotion. I bet that's just an excuse so you can be out longer and see your fancy man!'

Jody tried – in vain - to convince Tony he was wrong. It didn't matter what he was saying, he would not listen. Soon, Tony accused Jody of cheating every night as soon as she got in from work. It got so bad he would ring her work constantly and demand to speak to her, to prove she was actually there. He made Jody strip as soon as she got in, so he could check her for any telltale signs she had been with another man. Her sweet, loving boyfriend had disappeared, and instead she was left with a possessive and paranoid boyfriend.

Jody became withdrawn and dreaded going home. She couldn't live like that. It was taking its toll and she finally had enough.

'I can't do this anymore Tony. You need to leave.'

'I love you! I can't live without you.'

'This isn't love Tony. I can't live like this anymore. Please, just go.'

Jody went to walk away but Tony got up first and ran to the kitchen. He came back with a knife. At first Jody feared for her safety but Tony didn't want to hurt her, he placed the knife firmly against his wrist.

'I would rather die than live without you. You mean everything to me, Jody. Please give me another chance! I'll go to therapy, I'll get any help you think I need, just please don't leave me.'

Jody was at a loss. What could she do? What should she do? Jody knew things had to change but she didn't want Tony dead. Maybe this was the wakeup call he needed. Maybe now he understood how he had been treating her was wrong and she would have the fun, loving, sweet boyfriend she once had back. He had simply lost his way, but now he would get back to how he once was.

Something changed in Tony. when Jody got home from work the next night, she walked into a spotless flat. There were fresh flowers in the living room and kitchen, she could smell food cooking and there was a hot bath waiting for her. Tony came out of the bathroom, he was clean shaven and smelled delicious.

'I've been such an idiot, I could have lost you. I just wanted to spend all day, every day with you and I went a bit crazy. But I promise that had all stopped. I have some news. I found a new job,' Tony took hold of Jody's hands as he continued, 'The only problem is it's up north which means I will only be home at weekends. I need to do this Jody. I need to prove to you, and myself, that I can be the man you fell in love with.'

Jody was shocked, she hadn't expected anything like this. She was happy for him though, it was good to see him smile again. Jody knew she would support him, he needed to do this, to get out of the rut he had found himself in and to better himself so he could become the man he once was again.

They spent the next 4 days making love every chance they got and talking non-stop about how different things were going to be. They talked about what they would do at the weekends, about how much they would miss each other and about how great it was Tony was making a change. They were finally getting back on track and Jody could once again see herself having a happy life with Tony.

2 weeks later Tony broke up with her. By text! He then proceeded to block her number and easily removed her from his life. At first Jody was upset. After everything she had put up with, giving him every chance and helping him in every way she could, he just gets rid of her like she was nothing. That hurt. But then Jody realised it was actually a blessing. This was her lucky escape and Jody grabbed at it with both hands.

Then she discovered she was pregnant.

Jody knew the right thing to do would have been to get hold of Tony somehow and tell him about the baby, but she never even tried. The more she thought about it, the more she realised they would be far better off without him in their lives. Jody refused to risk him teaching their baby his behaviour was ok. No child should be made to think what he did was acceptable and the right way to live.

Jody never regretted her decision not to tell Tony. Until now.

Tony was shocked to see Jody. She was the last person he expected to see, he hadn't thought about her since he left. She had turned out not to be the wife material he thought she was. Tony expected his women to wait on him hand and foot, to see to his every want and need and to keep a clean home with food ready for him when he wanted some.

At first Jody was great, she had ticked all the boxes. Then Tony quit his job to really test just how good a wife she would make, and she failed. Terribly failed. Sex was great, she got full marks for that but that was it. Everything else she failed spectacularly at. He tried to help, he really did. He kept on at her to quit her job – which would give her more time to clean and see to his needs – but she was stubborn and wanted to be independent. This had been attractive at first, but Tony realised it wouldn't work, not when she had an attitude like that.

His new girlfriend Julie, had it right. She was up early every morning – always before him – to make herself look pretty and have his breakfast ready. She kept their place spotless and never nagged him to help out, no matter how messy he was. She could cook and was always willing to drop everything and make him whatever he wanted when he wanted it. She only left to get shopping and was always back before her allowed time ran out. If Jody had been more like Julie, their life would have been sweet.

It would be different now though. It was obvious Jody was pregnant – there was no mistaking that bump – and she had come to find him. The baby must be his and she had come to make things right between them. There was no other explanation. Once women had a taste of Tony, they always wanted more.

Jody would be better this time. More understanding of what was required from her, how things should be in a relationship. She would be a little lonely at first, but Tony would give her plenty of things to occupy her time and once the baby was born, she would long for boredom.

Last time he had held back from giving her a slap, he wouldn't be so nice this time around. She would need to learn quickly and do things correctly, they had a child now. He would mould her into the wife and mother she needed to be, by any means necessary.

Tony would chuck Julie, she was crap in the sack anyway. Jody would do better this time, she had tracked him down after all. She wanted him to help raise their baby. She wanted him to show her the right way. He would give her another chance and teach her the right way she should behave. Her stubbornness might kick up again, but he would get rid of it, he would beat it out of her if he had too. They would be happy this time.

Bless her, she looked so worried. After all she had done to track him down, she must be worried he would say no because of how she once was. Jody kept looking around and Tony assumed she must be worried about him rejecting her in public. He decided there and then he would make it as easy as possible for her. She would be so happy.

'Jody sweetheart, I am so glad you came to find me.'

That one sentence gave Jody shivers. She had feared this would happen when she saw him looking at her bump. She needed to knock this on the head right now.

'I'm not here for you Tony. I'm here for work.'

Bless her little heart, she was willing to make up lies rather than face his rejection in public. Tony felt sorry for her. He would make her see all was ok, he had forgiven her.

'Darling there is no need for all this pretence, I forgive you. I will give you another chance. We can be a family.'

Jody wished she could turn and run, but she couldn't, she was waiting for someone.

Marcus came out of the bank and spotted Jody straight away. It was her body language that got his attention. It was screaming to be left alone, but the man opposite her just wasn't getting it. He was completely oblivious to the discomfort he was causing her. Marcus wondered at the stupidity of his own gender sometimes.

Marcus walked over and stood next to Jody, facing Tony.

'Sorry I took so long, the queue was horrendous in the bank. Did I miss anything?'

'That's ok hunny, you're here now and no you didn't miss anything,' Jody said as she took a step closer to Marcus.

Tony understood now. Jody was a slut. He had been right about her all along and did the right thing when he dumped her skank ass. She must have jumped into bed with the first man that showed her a bit of attention. To think, he had been willing to give her another chance. He had been willing to mould her into a decent wife, someone worthy of him. Well, he just had a lucky escape. Once a slut, always a slut.

'Hello, I'm Marcus,' Marcus extended his hand to Tony.

Tony realised what was going on. Jody thought she could upset him, try to make him regret dumping her. She had tracked him down alright but not because of the baby, she wanted to rub her new sucker in his face. As if! Tony was far better than this dinlo and much too good for Jody. The dinlo was welcome to the slut. But if she thought he was going to let her get away with the audacity of it all, she was mistaken, and he would show her who was boss.

'Hello, I'm Tony,' he said to Marcus.

'It didn't take you long to move on,' Tony said to Jody in an accusing tone.

Jody wasn't the same person anymore, she no longer wanted to please Tony. Jody looked Tony in his eyes and with strength in her voice she replied, 'This from the guy who was shacked up with someone else within 2 weeks.'

This was further proof of Tony's lucky escape. Jody would never make a good wife when she was willing to back talk him, and in public no less! He was not about to let her get away with it. No woman would ever show him up, especially in public.

'Calm down woman. You're making a scene and embarrassing yourself,'

'No, I'm embarrassing you and I don't care.'

The relief Jody felt was immense. Jody felt her body relax as she stood up to Tony for the first time. Jody had been so scared of bumping into Tony, of falling back into the old pattern and letting Tony easily control her once more. It wasn't until he left that Jody realised just how much Tony had controlled her almost every aspect of her life. She had been terrified of becoming the meek, pleasing girl she had once been when around him, but after today she knew she had finally moved on. She no longer feared him. She no longer felt a deep need to make him happy, and she knew she was far better off without him. She was finally free of him and was more than willing to make sure he knew that.

Tony was livid. Who the fuck did she think she was? The slut thought she could speak to him like, belittle him and talk back to him. Try to humiliate him, and in public no less! He wouldn't stand for it, he would knock her into next week right now if he had too.

Marcus saw the look of anger and hatred in Tony's eyes and didn't like where it could be headed.

'Well it was nice to meet you Tony, but we really must be

going now,' Marcus took Jody's hand and took a step in the other direction, away from Tony.

Jody thought about staying, about making it very clear to Tony just how she felt. She wanted to verbally give him what for and enjoy the look she knew would appear on his face. There was something in Marcus's demeaner that stopped her. She had made her point. There was no need to give Tony anymore power over her. Jody turned her back on Tony and walked away with Marcus.

Tony stood for a few seconds, debating whether or not to go after them and give Jody a slap. He decided against it. She wasn't worth it, and he had he had another pregnant woman to see too. Julie was pregnant and wife material, she was what Jody should aspire to be like. Marcus was welcome to Jody, Tony had a real winner already. Life was good.

Marcus and Jody walked until they were sure Tony couldn't see them anymore. They stopped and looked back, Tony was headed in the opposite direction. It was over. Jody had had her worst fear thrust upon her and she had overcome it. She had proved to herself she was stronger now. Jody turned to the stranger who had helped her.

'Thanks for that, you didn't have to get involved.'

'Nonsense! I could see you needed help and what type of person would I be if I left a damsel in distress?'

Jody laughed. It felt good.

'Well thank you again anyway. I'm Jody by the way'

'Hello Jody, I'm Marcus.'

Jody noticed her boss looking for her, she waved her hand and shouted. He headed in her direction. Marcus said his goodbyes and left. Jody felt good, it was a nice feeling knowing there were still some decent men out there.

Jody had found out that morning she was having a baby boy. She had been unable to decide a name but now she had the perfect name. Marcus had a nice ring to it.

RING, RING, LET'S PLAY

Why did she let Debbie talk her into this? A blind date of all things, she must be mad!

Wendy had no luck with the opposite sex. Fairy tales had ruined her, men were not like that in real life. Men no longer opened doors, help out chairs or anything like that anymore. Men only did something when they wanted – or worse expected – something in return. Once you dropped your knickers that was it, men were no longer interested. They had what they wanted, the only reason they paid you any attention. Wendy once held strong onto the belief that were still a few good, decent men in the world, but she had learned the hard way, it wasn't true.

Wendy was no oil painting – as the old expression goes – but she was pretty, curvy, and more importantly, happy with how she looked. Modern chat up lines did nothing for her and she was the first to admit she could sometimes come across as standoffish and a bit of a prude without meaning too. Did that mean she only has herself to blame? Was she expecting too much? Was asking for a man she could trust, laugh with and be herself around really asking for too much?

Her friends seemed to think so. They said she was too picky, she needed to lower her standards. Wendy would rather be single forever than do that. Wendy wanted love, not to settle just so she could say she was in a relationship. If single life was her destiny forever then so be it, Wendy didn't need a man to complete her or to justify her existence. Besides, there are other ways to scratch the itch when it arises.

It was Wendy's job which started it all off with Debbie. Wendy worked from home and nobody knew exactly what she did. People assumed it was something like cold calling but that was nowhere near the truth. Wendy worked long hours – because she loved her job and set her own hours – this however, led those closest to her to believe she must be lonely. She must be desperate for a man and was burying herself in her work to cope. All untrue, but nobody would listen to her. All Wendy's friends had someone, and they couldn't understand – or refused to believe – how she could be happy by herself. Hence the blind date. It had been Debbie's idea. She had insisted. Wendy wasn't impressed – or interested – but it was easier to just go along with it. If nothing else, it would be an interesting evening.

Wendy was having trouble figuring out what to wear. She never dressed up – it wasn't her way – but she knew if she went in her usual getup, she would never hear the end of it. Smart casual was what she was aiming for, she hoped she had it right, matching clothes was not one of her strong points.

Wendy pinned a rose to her top, Debbie had insisted they both wear a rose for identification. Wendy couldn't decide if that was romantic or corny but went along with it anyway. Wendy checked herself for the last time and everything looked ok, if not, then tough, she didn't want to do this anyway.

Wendy put a jacket on then went out to her car. They had agreed to meet in a pub a short distance away, but Wendy took her car anyway, the last thing she wanted was to be followed home if it all went pear shaped. Wendy may not be as experienced as many, but she wasn't stupid.

Wendy stood outside the pub, she was hoping for a sneaky peek at her date before she went in. The pub was her local and a lovely place, great friendly atmosphere. Real oak tables and chairs, visible wood beams and an authentic rustic feel. Staff who made you feel welcome and appreciated, a valued customer. Wendy always enjoyed going there.

There was only one man with a rose on his jacket. He was attractive, dressed smartly and Wendy could see an expensive watch, so he wasn't short a few bob. He was sat, looking around and tapped his fingers on the table in frustration. Wendy checked her watch, she was still early. Not a good sign, maybe the evening wouldn't be as interesting as Wendy had hoped. There was nobody else around, nobody lingering nearby nervously wanting to go in, no cars pulling in to the pub carpark, no cars passing by at all. There was nothing else for it, Wendy took a deep breath and went in.

Lucas was getting impatient. He hoped this Wendy woman wasn't one of those infuriating women who believe it was their prerogative to be late for everything. He already knew she wouldn't be sexy, she had been described as having a great personality which equalled ugly. It could be worse, she could have been described as bubbly which equalled fat. Lucas did not do fatties.

Lucas was only on this stupid blind date to get his mother off his back. She had it in her head that he needed to find someone, should be looking for that special lady to settle down with. His mother wanted that, he did not. Lucas was still young and a man, so no biological ticking clock to worry about. Lucas had movie star looks, owned a very successful business, and owned 3 homes. He went on exotic holidays at least twice a year and made sure he always had the very best. The woman who would be lucky enough to have him, would also be the very best. Lucas had a list of requirements – all measurements – for his ideal woman. She would have to match the list exactly, or she would have no chance. Lucas had all the time in the world and wasn't interested in settling for someone ugly woman with a great personality. Who cared about personality anyway? Not Lucas.

Lucas was getting more impatient with every passing second. He already knew Wendy would not match his list and just wanted this evening over with so he could get his mother off his back for a few more months. Lucas loved his mother dearly, but she lived in a different time and only from a female perspective.

Finally Lucas saw a woman headed his way, this blind date could finally get underway and in good spirits Lucas decided to be very generous and give her an 8.

Wendy had stayed outside for a few more minutes, trying to decide if she should continue with the blind date or just go home. From outside she could see Lucas was attractive, but she could also see glaring bad traits. He was impatient and had no qualms in letting everybody know it. He glanced – sometimes glared – at passing woman and found them all lacking. Wendy had been told Lucas was successful, ambitious, and looking to find Miss Right. Wendy couldn't speak on the first 2 but by the looks of it, he would never find Miss Right.

Wendy made her way towards Lucas, she could see the disappointment in his eyes. Wendy sat down. Lucas made attempt to stand up, there was no chivalry in him. It would be a long evening. Once again Wendy asked herself why had she let Debbie talk her into the blind date. Why did the older generation – and those in a relationship – assume a single woman must be lonely? Wendy did not ask to be set up. She did not ask for help in finding someone. Wendy made a mental note to be more assertive in her personal life as she was in her professional life.

Lucas looked at Wendy, he could see her more clearly once she sat opposite him. He had been very generous indeed when he gave her an 8. She was at least a size 14 – 2 sizes bigger than his ideal woman – and she had not sashayed over to him. In fact, the only thing she had going for her was her breasts. They were big and lovely. Lucas knew fatties had the best naturally large breasts, but he couldn't deal with the rest of the flab that came with them. Wendy was on the borderline, not quite a fatty but very close. If she played her cards right and did more to attract him then she might be lucky enough to spend a few hours with him later. He couldn't be fairer than that.

Wendy sat and waited for Lucas to look at her face. So far, he had looked over her body in every way, several times – always coming back to stare at her breasts – but not yet looked her right in her face. Right in her eyes. Her breasts were the only thing he seemed to be interested in. Wendy wanted the date to be over, but

Lucas hadn't made a move to leave so she remained. She was also curious to see how it would end.

While on a date, Wendy had been told – more than once – it was customary for the woman to be careful what she ate. The food must be dainty – starve herself – and she must take minuscule bites. As the date was obviously a bust, Wendy ignored all that and ordered herself a steak with all the trimmings. If nothing else, she would have a decent meal from the evening.

Lucas was appalled. Did she not know it was un-lady like to order such a meal on a date? She should have ordered a salad, if not to impress him – which she should want to do anyway – then because she could clearly do with eating more salad. She was extremely close to becoming a fatty and was not helping herself. It amazed Lucas, how many woman still didn't get it. Men don't want inner beauty, they want eye candy. Something they can see, touch, and show off, not something they have to search for.

It was quiet at their table. Too quiet. All around them was noise. People laughed and chatted merrily. Staff talked and joked with customers and other staff. Sounds of plates clanging, drinks being poured, and glasses clinked together in celebration. The atmosphere was happy and jovial, everywhere except their table. They sat in silence.

Wendy had been on a few blind/set up dates in her life – friends and family always trying to "help" – but never one as bad as this. There had been Brian, who talked non-stop about his ex. Lewis, who kept touching himself. James, who kept touching every woman that went past. Colin, who stank so bad they had a whole section of the restaurant to themselves. Lastly, there was Ian, who just agreed with everything she said and seemed unable to decide anything for himself. Bad dates, wasted evenings, but they were great compared to Lucas.

When he did look up at her – very rare indeed – his eyes where full of disgust and disappointment. Wendy felt as if she had somehow insulted him, she hadn't even said a single word yet! At least with her other dates, there had always been a lesson, a clarity, something she could take from the experience. There was nothing with Lucas.

Small talk was not an option. If she were at home working, Wendy would be on top form, but in person, she was a shy woman. When she was working it was easier, she could release her inhibitions, play her deepest fantasies and be anybody she wanted to be. In person, Wendy shrunk inside herself, she didn't have the courage to talk first. Lucas no doubt didn't suffer from shyness, he just didn't want to talk to her.

Lucas was getting impatient again. Did his mother really thing this woman was a good match for him? She was nothing to look at – even if she had made an effort she would not be enough – but at least then he would have given her credit, maybe an extra point. As it was, she sat there waiting – expecting – him to start up a conversation with her and put her at ease. As if! He was stuck there looking at her, wasting his evening with her when he could be doing better things. He could be at a strip club or hook up with one of his many admirers. Anything would be better. He could even be at home, on the phone to Mrs X. Now there was a real woman, she understood him. But no, he was stuck in this crap hole with a boring 4 at best. If he had to suffer and be bored shitless then so would she, at least she got to look at him.

Their uncomfortable silence was broken – briefly – when their food arrived. The waitress set about her work – placing plates and checking if they wanted sauces etc – it was the most noise that had been made at their table since Wendy sat down.

It was obvious to everyone – Wendy was sure the other people could also see – the date was a complete bust, Wendy had enough and tucked into her meal. Wendy no longer cared if she appeared lady like or not. What did that even mean anyway? She was a lady so everything she did was lady like. She didn't use her fingers, or belch, how else was she meant to eat? Wendy pondered these questions and smiled to herself. She closed her eyes to better enjoy her meal – Lucas's sour face was putting her off – if nothing else, Wendy would make sure she enjoyed her meal. It was delicious, it always was.

Wendy decided there and then this would be her last blind

date. Each one had been more uncomfortable than the last but this one really took the piss. It was obvious Debbie had never met Lucas, if she had then all this could have been avoided.

The food was finished, their plates cleared and their glasses empty. There was nothing else to do, no other reason to prolong the evening. At this point in a good date, they would be arranging a second date and maybe contemplating extending the evening, not this date. Tonight, they wanted gone, both couldn't wait to get out.

Both stood up and put their coats/jackets on. Lucas was ahead and marched over to the bar. He demanded the bill, then went through it to find his orders. Lucas deliberately went through the bill and made sure everyone in earshot knew he was only going to pay for his items. Wendy was unsure if he was doing it because he always did it, or if he trying to embarrass her. She leaned towards natural for him but couldn't be sure. Wendy paid her share then headed to the doors.

It was when she had almost reached the exit doors that Wendy smiled. Lucas saw someone he knew and went over to say hello, and his voice rang in her ears. It was the way he said hello, she would know that voice anywhere. Wendy walked out the pub smiling to herself, what were the odds.

Lucas was puzzled as he saw Wendy smile. What was she smiling about? The date had been a complete disaster from the very beginning, and he had made sure she – and everyone else – knew just how disappointed he was. So why was she smiling? She actually had a rather pleasing smile if she had smiled earlier she would have been closer to getting lucky with him. Her loss.

Hopefully, Lucas would be able to salvage something of the evening. Mrs X was off for the evening, but Lucas doubted it would all night, he would stay up and wait until she came back online if he had too. She understood him. She was seductive, classy, and knew just what he liked. Lucas had to get back home, to see if he could make this evening better sooner. Lucas practically ran outside and to his car.

Wendy laughed as she watched Lucas quick pace to his car

and drive away at full speed. If only he had tried more, the evening would have gone much better. If he knew who she really was, it would have blown his mind. Just one reason why Wendy kept her real identity secret and used a professional name.

Wendy pulled up outside her house and went in. She took her coat off and went to the back room which she affectionately called her office. She got in her swivel chair, made sure she was comfy, then turned her computer on. It took a few seconds but then she was online. A few more minutes and she was logged into her work website. Wendy reached out and put on her headset, adjusted them then logged in.

Wendy waited for the call, she knew was coming. It had been 2 years since she first started her job. Wendy started as a cold caller, that led to other things, and eventually she ended up in her current job.

A sex operator.

Her friends and family thought she still did something to do with cold calling. Her calls were anything but cold! When Wendy had her headset on, she was a different person. Gone was the shy, prudish woman who dreams of prince charming. Replaced with a seductive, hearty woman who could make men come with her voice alone. Wendy was able to explore her sexual side without the need to sleep with half the male population. It was a win as far as Wendy was concerned.

As with any job, Wendy had her regulars. One in particular rang every night – without fail – and Wendy was expecting his call any minute now.

The caller icon appeared on the screen. Wendy clicked the green button and the call was connected. His voice came in loud and clear.

'Hello, Mrs X, you would not believe the terrible evening I have had. I really need your assistance.'

Wendy smiled, she would know that voice anywhere.

'It's ok Lucas, I'm here.'

THE PARK

A warm, lovely day with a light breeze. A quiet and peaceful part of town. Open fields. Children laughing, and dogs on leads chasing wild balls. Black iron gates announced the entrance to the park. It was the perfect place to spend her lunch break from work, and usually it always cheered Jane up. Not today.

Today Jane was in a mood and it couldn't be shifted. Her moron of a boss had just dumped the news on her that she would be working the weekend. Her birthday weekend, which she had booked off months ago in advance. The reason? He was having a BBQ and didn't want to do the shift himself. He was a waste of space. He was a useless, incompetent boss with the worst people skills she had ever come cross.

Jane asked herself the same question – for the ninth time that day alone – why didn't she just quit and be done with it? The answer was always the same. She had no special skills and a toddler that needed feeding, cleaning, clothing, heating and generally looked after. It was a typical dead-end job, minimum wage with rubbish hours and no respect from management. There was no guarantee another job would be any better. A new boss could be better, or worse. She could get more respect at a new job, or just as bad as she had it now. There was no way to tell and as the old saying goes, "It's better the devil you know."

Jane was so preoccupied she almost tripped over a Staffy that was dragging a man holding onto its leash.

The man was Michael, and it wasn't his dog. The dog belonged to his boyfriend, who was still hiding in the closet. Oh he was gorgeous, funny, smart, and amazing in bed, but also scared. Too scared to be out in the open and Michael was getting sick of it. Michael was lucky, he knew that. His family had guessed he was gay from an early age, so when he had finally plucked up enough courage to tell them, they had already accepted him years ago. There had been no backlash. No disownment or hatred thrown his way. Nobody suggested it was phase or the latest fad and he would grow out of it. There was no hint of shame or embarrassment. His parents never asked where they had gone wrong or that he just hadn't met the right girl yet.

He had been extremely luck, and he knew that. He understand his boyfriend's fear, it could have gone so much worse for him when he came out. He just couldn't remain the "roommate" forever. He was loved – and desired – but he couldn't remain the dirty secret. When his boyfriend had visitors Michael was relegated to his room – only time it was his room – and not allowed to be part of anything. Michael couldn't live like that much longer, but he didn't want to leave. That's where the problem was.

The dog had been his boyfriend's idea. Only straight, tough men had Staffies. It would put doubts/questions about his sexuality on the back burner. At least, his boyfriend thought so. Michael told him it was nonsense, but his words fell on deaf ears. It couldn't go on like this forever, something had to change.

The dog was a bloody nightmare and began pulling Michael along again, trying – in vain – to catch a squirrel running up a tree.

Tony watched the man get dragged along by the big dog and laughed at the man's obvious stupidity. The dog must be a female – in his opinion – as they are always dragging men around, and down. It was the same for all animals, humans especially. The lion may be the king of the jungle, but he was still whipped by the lioness. It was no different for humans, men were superior in every way, but women ruled them. When had they all become such wimps? Why did they allow women to control them, when had they? Men were warriors! Men were superior! Men were rulers! And yet, they had allowed women to take over.

Tony saw it every day, in every aspect of his life, and it sickened him. He was his own man and would never let any female – human or otherwise – to tell him what he could and couldn't do.

It was the reason he could never hold down a job. Too many mouthy lasses in the workplace. They had been allowed to reach up higher on the ladder than they ever should have been. It was just plain wrong.

Why couldn't anybody else see it? Surely, he couldn't be the only person who saw it, who understood the damage they were doing to their race by allowing it to happen. Feminism was to blame for it all. Men had given in and given woman a little bit of extra room, and woman had taken that generosity and dug out an entire empire. Men had done nothing. Men had thought it funny, had allowed women to run with it, and now there was chaos. Feminism had taken over and men were too scared to take control back.

The world was sinking – thanks to women thinking were equal to men – and he was the person who could see it. Tony sat on the bench and wrote in his notebook, he needed to get it all down, to make sure that one day the world understood where it had gone wrong and who was to blame.

Sally walked past the bench. The man sitting on it gave her a filthy look, she was tempted to confront him about it, but his frantic scribbles told her he was messed up enough. Besides, Sally was on cloud 9 and didn't want to let anyone ruin it, especially a looney toons like the man on the bench.

She had done the test 4 times and the result was the same each time. Positive. Sally was pregnant. Almost 3 years of trying and it had finally happened. Sally wanted to keep it a secret – she didn't want to jinx it – but she was so excited about it, she expected everyone to be able to guess by her inner glow. Sally had made an appointment that morning, and in a few weeks she would have her first ever midwife appointment.

Fear was creeping up inside her though, and as much as she tried to ignore, she couldn't. 3 years of trying, 2 false pregnancies and utter heartbreak can take its toll. Sally was terrified something would go wrong and her dream would be snatched away from her before it even fully began. It could happen at any time, without warning. The thought had been whirling around her head since the very first positive result. Sally tried to think positive, but the nagging doubts refused to stay away.

Thinking positively was all good and well in principle, but heartache, longing and dread for years could not just be dismissed and forgotten about that easily. Sally would continue to try though, she wanted to enjoy this moment, the whole experience and she would do everything she could to stop the negative thoughts from taking over.

Sally just had to hold out until after her first scan. Once she saw her beautiful baby she would be able to relax and let herself believe. Then she would tell closest to her the great news, talking about it would help relieve the pressure and reassure her.

Sally went back to cloud 9. She passed a lady sat on a bench with a little baby in her arms and smiled. That would soon be her.

Tasha smiled at the lady as she walked past. Tasha recognised the look and was about to call out to congratulate her when her little bundle of joy started to whimper. Tasha held Oscar up to face him and blew raspberries on his cheeks. She was rewarded with giggles. Doctors say he is too young to giggle, but Tasha ignored them. Her son was giggling, and it was the best sound in the world.

Oscar wasn't planned – the result of a one-night stand – but Tasha regretted nothing. Ok, maybe the stretch marks and the pain of labour, but nothing to do with keeping Oscar.

Her mum hadn't been pleased. She had flipped her lid, said she was disappointed in her, called her a few unpleasant names and then kicked Tasha out. There was no help from her so called friends or family. It was ridiculous, but also scary.

Tasha had been 4 months pregnant when she was forced to leave. 7 months later, and Tasha sat in the park waiting to see her mum again for the first time. Tasha's mum had called out of the blue – Tasha kept her same number – apologised and said she wanted to make things up, get back as a family. It had been different when she was younger – her mum explained – and it had been a terrible shock. She deeply regretted how she reacted and wanted to make amends.

Her mum had been crying on the phone and Tasha instantly softened. Tasha had agreed to meet and hoped she was doing the right thing, she missed her mum dreadfully. Oscar began whimpering again – he could sense her tension – and Tasha lost herself in entertaining him. Her mum sat next to her and they both got lost in Oscar.

Jake watched the women blush at the baby and wondered if his mum would be the same. He was 15. He only had sex once, but now he was going to be a dad. How could this be happening? It had been over within seconds.

Mandy – his girlfriend – had said he was amazing, but it had been over so quickly. He had pulled out, how could she be pregnant. He believed her though, Mandy wasn't a liar.

Best friends since they were 2. Jake would trust Mandy with his life, which in effect, is exactly what he was doing. His mum would kill him. He was 15. How could he have been so stupid. So reckless. He was the oldest of 4 and should have set an example.

His mum had raised them all by herself, worked 2 jobs to scrap by and always made sure they were taken care of. Jake could feel the disappointment he would bring to his mum, and it saddened him. All he wanted was to make his mum proud. To show her, she had done an amazing job by them all. But he had messed up. He would be just another teenage dad, and people would blame his mum. It would be her fault for not raising him right, for no father figure in his life and all the other rubbish people say. He had made the choice, it was his fault. No matter how his mum reacts, Jake will not let anyone bad mouth her. He was wrong, not her.

Jake waited nervously for his mum to get back from the drinks truck. Once she had a nice cup of tea in her, he would tell her the news.

The park meant so much to Sandra. It was where she always went when she needed to clear her head or make a decision. And where she went when she wanted to hide. Like today. Sandra was hiding from making the most difficult decision of her life. Which family to keep, and which to lose forever. Her girlfriend or her dad.

Her mum was cool with her sexuality, not her dad. He said it was disgusting. She hadn't met the right man, and when she did, she would forget all about this nonsense. It was a phase and she would grow out of it. He was wrong but wouldn't listen. He gave her an ultimatum, and she had to choose.

Since a young girl, Sandra knew she was different from her sisters. She didn't know how, or why, just that she was. A niggling feeling that wouldn't go away.

When Carol came into her life, everything clicked. It sounds corny, but she really was the missing piece in Sandra's life. 8 blissful months together before her dad found out and all hell broke loose. Her dad had been livid. He blew up. Sandra could not have Carol and her dad in her life, she had to choose.

If Sandra chose her dad, he would never accept the real her. Carol did and would continue to always be there for her. Carol never made her choose. Carol never gave her an ultimatum. Carol accepted Sandra for who she truly was, her passions and little quirks as well.

Her choice had been made. Why had she taken so long to realise? Carol was her future, all she would need to truly be happy.

Carol was almost at the bench, Sandra still had time. She took off her promise ring and got down on one knee. Carol screamed in joy, shouted yes and ran to Sandra.

Jane walked past the happy couple on her way back out the iron gates, and back to work. Her lunch break over, Jane had to hurry back before her boss threatened her with the sack.

Jane always came in on short notice to cover shifts. Jane

always came in on her days off, or her booked holiday days. She always went in early and stayed late – without overtime – on a daily basis. Nothing mattered. "Nobody is irreplaceable," was her boss's favourite saying. He said it to her every day.

Once again she asked herself why she bothered. Why did she do the extra work when it was never appreciated? Once again, the answer was the same. She needed a job.

TRUE, HONEST CLOSURE

'Are you kidding me? You can't be serious!' Milo couldn't understand why Hamish would say this to it.

'Milo, buddy, you know it makes sense. It's been almost 2 years since you last spoke to her, but she is still under your skin. You need closure.'

That word again, closure. He had been hearing that word a lot lately, ever since Kerry reared her lying, cheating, selfish head again. Everybody kept telling him, he needed closure. But why? He doing just ignoring her existence, and he said as much.

'Yeah, when she was gone you was doing fine. Now she's back and wants you again, you hide away, and not just from her.'

This was true, but Milo still didn't want to see Kerry.

'I will grant you that, but why do I need to see her? All she will do is lie and try to worm her way back into my life,' this was said as fact and without self-pity. A statement of fact.

Hamish was worried about Milo. He had been spiralling downwards ever since Kerry reappeared. Hamish had never met Kerry, but she clearly had some kind of power over Milo, she could affect him without even seeing him. Milo needed to end it. Either give her another chance and try to make it work or do whatever he had to do to get her out of his life – and out of his system – forever.

Milo couldn't go on like he was. It was effecting his career. He knew he had to do something, but truth was, he was scared. He was scared of seeing her again and not being able to stop her getting her claws back in him. It would only end in his heartbreak all over again.

Milo was sick with nerves. In less than 10 minutes Kerry would walk through the front door, follow the rose petals and find Milo on his knee, right arm extended and holding an engagement ring. Milo had spent days thinking about the best way to propose, and several hours setting everything out just right. The closer she got to coming home, the more worried he became she would say no.

Milo's parents said it was too early, they had only been together 7 months. But Milo knew Kerry was the woman for him. Every morning Kerry was on his mind the second he woke up. He thought about Kerry every night as he slept. When they were apart, he felt a physical ache, and when they argued – which was very rare – he hurt. Kerry was in his bloody. Under his skin, and fully in his heart. Milo knew without a doubt, he would never love anybody the way he loved Kerry.

Kerry was the first woman Milo had ever truly opened up too, bared his soul too. Milo had given into his feelings and allowed happiness to take over. If Milo had to choose between Kerry and life itself, he would gladly die for her.

Many of his friends said he was whipped – especially as they had yet to make love – but Milo didn't see it like that. Kerry said she wanted to wait until they were married, and Milo respected that. Waking up next to her was enough.

Milo wanted everything to be perfect, he wanted the proposal to be worthy of any romantic film. Milo had thought of and taken care of everything.

Rose petals leading a trail from the front door to Milo – check.

Wine in an ice bucket – check.

Lasagne, Kerry's favourite, keeping warm in the oven – check.

Milo had even written a poem instead of a speech for Kerry.

It may be quick,
It may be soon,
You are the stars,
To my moon.

I just know,
Our love is true,
We can be whole,
Me and you.

I love you,
With all my heart,
Please be my wife,
And let our new life start.

Kerry would be home any minute. Milo was filled with nerves but also excitement. He just hoped she said yes.

Kerry was in a pickle. She had 2 men in love with her. Milo was technically her boyfriend, but Donny had more going for him. Milo was sweet, charismatic and treated her like a princess, but so did Donny. Plus, the sex with Donny was amazing. Milo was patient and Kerry appreciated that, but Donny had been so tempting, Kerry couldn't help herself. Kerry regretted nothing.

Now Donny wanted to take things further and live with Kerry. She already lived with Milo – Donny knew nothing about Milo – and so Kerry was in a pickle. What to do? Who to choose?

If she was honest, she had already picked Donny – she had already slept with him while making Milo wait – but she didn't want to give Milo up. She knew she should have ended it with Milo when she started dating Donny – or at least once she began sleeping with him – but she hadn't. Kerry had stayed with Milo and allowed him to fall deeper in love with her. Kerry loved the way Milo worshipped her, but Donny made her tingle.

Kerry decided to deal with it when the time came, for now, she would enjoy having them both for as long as she could.

The time was up.

Milo heard the front door open, then close. Milo heard a slight gasp before the living room door opened and Kerry stood in front of him, gobsmacked. One look at Kerry's face and all Milo's fears disappeared.

He smiled up at Kerry and read his poem. There were a few agonising seconds of silence before Kerry spoke. His fears resurfaced and Milo wanted to ground to open up and swallow him whole. He was wrong, Kerry said yes! Kerry fell into his arms, kissing him all over. Milo felt as if his heart would explode with happiness.

They spent the next few days talking about everything. They talked about wedding itself, colour schemes, possible dates, who to invite, places for the reception etc. They talked about the honeymoon, where to go, how long for, the type of honeymoon etc. And they talked about decorating their home, to make it theirs. They talked. They made lists. They even made a scrapbook full of ideas. It was bliss.

3 days later, Milo came home to an empty home. Kerry was gone. All she left was a not: I've found someone else. Don't contact me again. I don't want you.

That was it.

That's how she ended it. They had been a couple for 7 months, lived together for 4 months. Milo had paid for everything and did whatever Kerry wanted, whatever mad her happy. She gave no indication she was unhappy or had been looking elsewhere. She had said yes to marriage, then left within a few days. Milo was devastated. His life was shattered. He wanted to fade away and forget he was ever born.

Milo was a complete mess for months after Kerry left. He also, discovered many things about her, and her double life. Kerry had been with another man for almost as long as she had been with Milo. Kerry had made Milo wait but had happily slept with the other man. People thought Milo was just a roommate. It hurt.

Milo felt betrayed, but it made no difference. He would still have taken her back without a second's thought.

If it hadn't been for Milo's family and friends, he didn't know how he would have coped. He strongly believed he would not have coped. If left to his own devices, he would have shut himself off and let himself wither away. They saved him. They made him go out. They made him join in. They kept going to see him and involved him in everything they did, whether he liked it or not. They made him think about other things.

Almost 6 months after Kerry left him, one of his cousins wanted to propose to his girlfriend. His cousin, James, asked Milo for help. He knew – they all knew – Milo had talent and James wanted Milo's help with the proposal.

At first Milo refused. He thought it would hurt too much, but he changed his mind. Milo had always helped James in the past and didn't want his hurt to stop him helping others be happy. Milo wrote a poem especially for them. It was a huge success. She said yes and they married a year later. It help Milo immensely, he even wrote James another poem for him to read out at the reception.

Hamish was an independent talent agent, and a close personal friend of the bride. He had moved from Scotland, wanted to make his mark. He failed big time. That was until the wedding, it all changed when heard James's speech. It needed more work – a chorus and a few more versus – but then it would be perfect.

Hamish could sell it on as a song. Song lyrics were big business, Hamish knew he had found a talent. Hamish signed Milo up there and then. Milo didn't think it would go anywhere but he did think it would help him move on. It did. It was easy, steady work. Milo enjoyed it immensely.

Then one fateful night, a band sang a song he wrote on a national talent show. Overnight Milo became a household name. It was so successful, Hamish had to get another phone. Milo's hobby began to make him very rich. Milo found himself being followed by journalists, trying to get a story with the latest hottest news. It didn't last long. The press found something else after a few weeks.

One national newspaper took up the story about Milo. Funnily enough, that was when Kerry got back in contact. First, she tried ringing Milo, but he ignored her. She sent messages, but to no avail. Next, she started contacting Milo's friends and family, she was told to stay away but she didn't. Next, she started leaving messages on Milo's business site. Milo now had money, he was a well-known name, and he had always loved Kerry. Now Milo was perfect, Kerry wasn't going anywhere soon.

Milo agreed to meet Kerry. He knew he would have to eventually, so better to get it over with as soon as. He left Hamish to sort out the details. He didn't want more contact with Kerry than was needed.

Kerry hoped she wouldn't have to work too hard to get Milo back on her side. She didn't like to work for anything, and felt men should do the chasing, not her. Kerry had secretly kept check on Milo. He had been with a few women but not for long, and nothing serious. Rumour was, he was still hung up on and ex. This was good for Kerry. It meant she had a better chance. Kerry was still with Donny but as always, she was keeping her options open. Donny had no idea about Milo of course, he still had no idea they had been anything other than roommates. Donny had proposed a few months ago and Kerry had said yes. Then, a few weeks ago she read all about Milo and his newfound riches. He looked as good as ever. Kerry had chosen Donny because the sex was amazing, and he was financially better off than Milo had been. Milo had always loved and worshipped her – just how Kerry liked her men to be – and Kerry hoped he still did. Donny was in blissful ignorance, he thought Kerry loved him. Truth was that Kerry only loved herself. She loved men in general. Loved money and men spending money on her. Kerry loved sex. She loved being chased, admired and desired. But, Kerry only loved Kerry.

Kerry sat at the table in the hotel she had been told to sit at. Kerry had received a message from a man called Hamish, he was Milo's agent and had arranged everything. Donny thought Kerry was at her mum's. She would dump him like a dead weight once she had Milo hooked again, but until then there was no need to burn her bridge with Donny. Kerry ran through the lies she had concocted for Milo. He had fallen for her lies in the past, every time because he had wanted to believe them. He had had loved her so much he had been willing to believe anything if it meant they would be together.

Kerry was a pro: she would spin the wool right over his eyes and have him begging her to come back with days. Kerry knew she to grovel, but that was ok. She had practised, rehearsed and thought of every possible outcome. She always came out on top. Milo was her best bet for living the life she wanted – and felt she deserved – and she wasn't going to easily give that up.

Ever since she saw the paper "**Local lad writes songs for the stars**" she knew she had made a mistake. She could have been in the paper with Milo. She could have been spotted by someone. She could have had her chance to make it big, but she threw Milo away and lost her chance. That would change. Milo would soon be at the table with her and everything would be smooth sailing for Kerry from then on. Just like always. Kerry always looked out for Kerry, and Kerry always got what she wanted.

Hamish had arranged everything. The hotel was out of town – no chance of local journalists trying to take pictures – unlikely chances of bumping into anyone he knew. Hamish had arranged for a room in case things heated – argumentatively or sexually – and paid for the meals and room in advance, so Milo could just walk out without worry if it came to that. Hamish hoped he had done the right thing, pressuring Milo to meet Kerry. Hamish still believed Milo needed closure, but he was worried things would get worse for Milo. It was done now. Hamish and everyone else who loved Milo, would be there for him no matter what the outcome.

Milo sat in his car, in the underground carpark of the hotel. Nerves were a funny thing, they could push you to do great things or, like then, they could make you want to run and flee. The urge to turn on the ignition, reverse and leave was so strong that Milo had to put his keys in his pockets to stop himself. He had to do it. He knew Hamish was right. He had to get Kerry out of his system. They had never properly split. They were engaged and in love – or so he had thought – then Kerry was just gone. It was all of a sudden, and Milo hadn't expected a thing. He had never been able to move on properly. He only hoped, he could do that this time. He still loved Kerry and if he were honest, knew he always would. But, he also knew tonight would be full of lies and broken promises. He knew the truth about Kerry. He knew she was still with Donny. He knew she had gotten engaged to him recently. Milo knew it wasn't a coincident that Kerry had got back in contact as soon as Milo was making a name for himself. But the heart has a mind of its own and Milo needed to be strong. He needed to say no. He needed to get this over and done with. Milo got out of his car, locked it, and headed up to the restaurant.

Milo spotted Kerry as soon as the lift door opened. Her hair was shorter, she wore flashier clothes, but she looked almost the same as when he had last seen her. Milo walked over to her. He pulled out his chair and sat down opposite Kerry.

'Kerry,' he said with a nod as he pulled his chair in. Milo had no intentions of doing all the talking. Kerry wanted the meet: Kerry could work for it.

'I've missed you so much Milo,' Kerry sounded sincere. Kerry reached out for Milo's hand.

Milo had anticipated she would try something like that and moved his hand away. He laid his hands on his lap without a word.

'Milo, please don't be like that. I know I've hurt you. I know I was a bitch, but I want to make it right. I need to make it right. To make us right,' Kerry started crying. Milo could see tears in her eyes, then roll down her cheeks. His resolve was breaking. He needed to stay strong.

'Kerry I'm only here to tell you to stop. You made your choice and you have to leave me alone.'

'I can't! Don't you see? I love you Milo, I always have. My feelings for you were so strong I got scared. I didn't know how to handle them. They scared me and I ran away. I shouldn't have, and I wish I hadn't. Please give me another chance,' Kerry was crying so loudly the other guests in the restaurant where watching them.

Milo could do without the audience. People staring at them. Kerry crying her eyes out. His heart trying to burst through his chest. The urge to go to Kerry and to hold her was strong. Milo needed to stay strong, needed to get out of there. Milo didn't know what to do.

Kerry sensed his hesitation. She knew he was faltering. She had to make her move.

'Can we go somewhere quiet and really talk about things? I don't like everyone watching.'

Milo was a gentleman, even he had to admit he could not get closure like this.

'Hamish booked me a room in case I was in no fit state to drive home. He thought I might be too drunk from celebrating my life without you.'

It was a cheap shot – and he wasn't pleased with himself – but Milo needed to make it clear and stay strong. The cheap shot was a reminder to himself as well as her.

Milo walked out of the restaurant and over to the clerks desk. He got his room key and walked over to the lift. Kerry waited at the lift. They went in, and up in silence. Milo unlocked the door and went in, Kerry followed. As soon as Milo shut the door, Kerry started crying again. She needed to put the pressure on Milo. If she went too slow and soft, he would have more chance of getting away from her. Kerry couldn't risk him leaving. She wanted the life he could provide, and she would do whatever it took to get it. Kerry sat on the bed. She looked vulnerable. She looked hurt. Milo gave in. Milo couldn't bear to see Kerry like that, he went over to her and sat next to her but kept his hands to himself.

'Please stop crying. This doesn't have to end badly, but it does need to end Kerry. You broke my heart. You destroyed me, and I can't go through that again.'

'I know. I would give anything to take it all back if I could, but I can't. It's not possible. But I can do anything you want to make it up to you. I am begging you. Please Milo, give me another chance.'

Kerry moved in close and kissed Milo. He pulled back but Kerry kept moving closer until Milo was flat on the bed. Kerry climbed on top of Milo, she straddled him and covered him in passionate kisses. Milo tried to resist, but his heart and body overruled him. They made love. The moment Milo came, Kerry knew he was hers again. She snuggled up against his bare chest and fell asleep in his arms.

Milo had just begun to fall asleep when a beeping sound woke him up. He carefully slid Kerry off of him and found the source of the noise. It was Kerry's phone. As it flashed alight from another text, Milo realised he was now the other man. He was the bit on the side and Kerry would always be on the lookout for the next best thing. For another man to cling on too. He had known it already, but it had finally sunk in. He had the closure he needed. Now he could finally move on.

Milo got up. Got dressed and left a simple not for Kerry. It felt appropriate. Then he left. He still loved her, but he no longer had her under his skin. He was free of her.

BACK IN THE FAMILY

Margaret sat on the lounge chair and watched as Emily played in the sandpit. Emily was oblivious to being watched and was concentrating on building the biggest sandcastle she could. Margaret could – and would – watch her all day if she were given the chance. The last time Margaret saw Emily, she was only a few weeks old. She had changed so much.

When Emily was first born, she had tuffs of brown hair, now her hair was blonde. Bright blue eyes and looking more and more like her father every day.

Margaret felt a pang of guilt, and loss. Guilt because she had missed so much of Emily's life. Those first few years really were precious. First crawl, first walk, first smile. They were lost to Margaret forever, but she could still make new firsts. First time to babysit Emily by herself. First time to take her for a day out by herself. Most precious day of all, when Emily runs up to her, excited to see her and shouting nanny.

Emily was the bright spark in her life, and the only link she had left of her son. Mark had been a handful growing up, always in trouble at school and causing Margaret hassle with the neighbours. As an only child, Margaret admitted she spoiled him and always jumped to his defence, even when she knew he was in the wrong. She let him get away with many things she never should have. She enabled him to be the worst version of himself. Margaret lost family and friends because she always sided with her son. It did not matter what he did, he was her son and all she had. Margaret could now admit her son had not turned out to be very nice, but he was all she had, and she loved him dearly.

Mark had begun to change his life around once he met Julie. It was subtle little things, but they were very clear to Margaret, and she was pleased. Little by little, he was becoming a nicer, politer, kinder person. Margaret was very pleased with the change, and then he was taken away from her.

Mark had got his life together. He still had some bad habits, but he was working on them and that was amazing. Margaret had tried for years to make him see sense, but he never listened. Until Julie came along. He then stopped gambling, stopped fighting, and cut down on his drink. He no longer did drugs and was much more pleasant to be around. Margaret was thrilled. Her mark had finally become a decent man. A son to be proud of.

If only he had managed to cut the drink out completely, he would still be with them. He just had to have that last drink at the weekend, and stupidly drove his motorbike. Margaret wasn't there for the crash itself, but she read the police report and knew it was Mark's fault. He was over the limit. He was swerving in and out of traffic, dodging through vehicles. He did all that when sober, but because he was drunk, he misjudged the gap between 2 cars. Mark was going too fast and as the car in front of him moved to the left, Mark swerved, lost control of the bike and drove straight into a tree. There was no hope. He died before paramedics arrived.

After the car crash – which took him away from her – Margaret had been left feeling as if she had nothing left in the world. Mark had been her life for so long. Time, money, energy always focused on Mark. From a very early age Margaret had known she wanted to be a mum. Years of trying had resulted in failed attempt after failed attempt to conceive. Finally, Margaret had given up, then had fallen pregnant. The pregnancy and labour had not been kind to Margaret, but once she had her precious son in her arms, she would gladly do it all over again. It had remained like that ever since. There was nothing Margaret would not have done to make her son happy. Including buying him the bike he was killed on.

For so long after the crash Margaret blamed herself for buying him the bike. Blamed the bike manufacturer, and anyone and anything else she could for his death. She couldn't stand the idea of blaming Mark. Margaret sank low into despair; it was over a year before she came back up for air. Julie had saved her. Margaret had shut herself away from everything and everyone. Including her precious granddaughter. Julie had called out of the blue, begged Margaret to come and see Emily. It had been the wakeup call Margaret needed. Nothing was going to bring back Mark, but the thought of missing more of Emily's life, filled Margaret with dread.

Margaret began therapy. She couldn't be a part of Emily's life the way she was. Margaret needed to get out from under the cloud of despair she stuck under. Margaret needed to finally accept things for how they were. She couldn't change the past, but she had to see it clearly.

It took a few months, but finally Margaret could venture outside again without feeling the black cloud above.

Today was the first day Margaret had seen Emily since she was a few weeks old. Her resemblance to her father was both painful and pleasing at the same time. Her Mark was not completely gone. He would have been so proud of Emily, and how Julie was raising her. Mark could not be there himself, but Margaret swore to get herself together so she could be.

Emily was in a world of her own. She sat happily in her sandpit in the back garden and laughed as she hit her spade down on her castle, crumbling it. Margaret laughed as she watched. Margaret wished she could turn back the clock and be there for Emily and Julie since the crash. Margaret had regrets, but Julie was a diamond. Margaret had no idea where she would be today if it hadn't been for Julie. Mark may not have done many right things in his life, but he had struck gold when he met and stayed with Julie.

Julie had saved Mark, and then Margaret.

WEB, SURF, LOVE

It was almost complete, just one more thing to do. Sylvia gave the page one last look over, made sure all the details were correct and her picture was in focus, upright and looked cheerful. Then pressed done. A few seconds later and Sylvia was informed her dating profile was up and running. Sylvia had never felt comfortable going to clubs, and as for making the first move – asking someone out, flirting – well forget about it. Sylvia was shy, introverted. That's why internet dating was such a great idea.

Sylvia could take her time, get to know any potential partners before meeting them – hopefully, it came to that – and best of all, any unwanted suitors could be blocked. No leeches or pervs trying to touch her up while she waited for a drink. She didn't have to try to be more confident than she was or worry about dressing up every time she wanted a chat. Internet dating made finding your true love – or at least a decent frog – much more relaxing and comfortable for those afflicted with severe shyness such as Sylvia.

Sylvia's best friend Tammy wasn't sure about internet dating. Tammy could understand the appeal, though she never had a problem meeting anyone herself. Tammy had been amazed at Sylvia's shyness. Sylvia became a very different person around men – those she liked, or those who made a pass at her – it wasn't a nice change. Tammy was great at reading body language and was a well-known, notorious flirt, but Sylvia didn't have a clue. Sylvia was completely oblivious, so Tammy could understand the appeal for those as shy as Sylvia. Tammy just didn't like it. Too many horror stories about online dating.

'Are you sure about this? What if you come across a nutter?' Tammy asked with concern. Sylvia's safety was very important to Tammy, she knew what Sylvia had been through in her life. Sylvia knew Tammy meant well but she wished she would let it drop. They had been over this many times already.

'I could meet a nutter at a club, on the street or even through an unsuspecting friend. Nutters are everywhere, we meet them all the time, not just online.'

'But it makes it easier for them,' Tammy wanted to make sure her friend really understood the possible dangers. The internet just made everything so much easier for anyone with ill intent.

'True, but the phone makes it easier for nutters as well, and binoculars, cameras and recorders of any kind make things easier for stalkers, nutters and blackmailers but we still use all those things,' Sylvia turned and looked her friend fully in the face, 'look mate, I know you're worried, but I will be fine. I won't give out my address or my phone number, and if I arrange to meet anyone I will tell you so you can be my hidden security.'

Tammy liked the sound of that and felt better about Sylvia's security. Sylvia was a smart and sensible woman, she deserved happiness. Sylvia was a great catch, funny, loving, sweet, and when she felt truly comfortable, she could be the life and soul at any get together. Tammy hoped it would all work out.

Tammy was curious about it all. She sat closer to Sylvia and they scrolled down the page on the site. Sylvia concentrated her search on those who lived in her local area. There were several to choose from. Sylvia clicked on one to take a better look and was very pleased with what she saw. Tammy, however, had doubts again. The man seemed too good to be true, which usually meant he either didn't exist or worse.

'How do you know this guy is real? He could be lying through his teeth. He sounds too good to be true, so most likely is.'

Sylvia loved Tammy, but she was starting to get on her

nerves. Sylvia understood where Tammy was coming from, and why she was saying these things, but enough was enough. They had been over it so many times and Sylvia was getting annoyed at keep repeating herself. To justify herself to her best friend.

'He could be yes, but so could anybody I met outside in the real world. This guy,' Sylvia pointed to the screen which was still on the man's profile, 'could be lying about everything, but so could anybody else. Anyone can lie about their age, their job, if they are single or not, if they have children or not etc. The only difference is that in person I can see what the person looks like whereas, online it's just a picture. Then again, there is hair dye, fake coloured lenses and make up to disguise how someone really looks.'

Tammy had to admit Sylvia had a point. Almost everyone seemed to be changing something about their appearance these days for vanity reasons alone.

'If somebody is a liar then they will lie. The internet doesn't make an honest, decent person suddenly turn into a liar. Same with being a cheat or nutter. We say it all the time when we hear about a social network getting the blame for a partner cheating. It had nothing to do with the site. That person chose to cheat, the site didn't make them do it.'

Again, Tammy had to admit Sylvia had a point. It was clear Sylvia had thought it all through and was not about to change her mind. Sylvia could be stubborn when the mood took her. Tammy decided it would be best to just keep her fingers crossed on her friend's behalf and be there for her if she was needed.

Sylvia had been on the dating site for 2 months before Kev found out. He was furious at the news. What was she playing at? She belonged to him! Their love was inescapable. She was bound to him forever. It was beyond a joke, and he would find a way to put a stop to it. She had the audacity to think she could get away with something like that. She gave her heart to him and, in his book, that meant she was his forever. It made no difference they were apart or that he didn't love her, she gave her heart so belonged to him until he said otherwise.

Kev had found Sylvia's profile by accident. He was on so many different dating sites, he often forgot which one's he had checked recently. It could get very confusing sometimes, but it was worth it in the long run. When Kev had checked the site, it had shown Sylvia as a new match. Kev never used a picture on any of his profiles – he would send them a picture of himself when the lady was hooked – so he was not worried about Sylvia recognising him. He could not believe his Sylvia was whoring herself out. Putting it around for fuck knows who. It was normal – expected even – for a man to spread it around and have a bit on the side, but not a woman! It wasn't right. She was one of his women and he would not stand for it!

The past 2 months on the dating site had been a learning curve for Sylvia. For some men "want to suck my cock" or "I want your pussy" or "I bet you have great tits" and even cruder comments, seemed perfectly acceptable first message. No hello how are you. Or, hi my name is …. Or, hello I liked your profile, care to chat?

The site did not allow pictures to be sent unless both parties had already sent and responded in a message first. Sylvia suspected it was the only reason why she hadn't been inundated with unwanted dick pics as well. She was thankful the site had that safety measure.

Then there were the men even shyer than herself, trying to get a conversation out of them was harder than trying to build a house with one hand tied your back. Sylvia tried telling jokes, asking them questions in the hope of getting them to open up etc, but she was lucky if they even replied with more than one word.

Sylvia gave up on them as well. Sylvia was shy, but it was different online. She didn't have anyone staring at her while she thought of a reply. She could be herself and communicate better. If the men couldn't even hold a conversation online, how did they expect to cope when on a real date?

It wasn't all bad though. Sylvia did not want to give up on

the online dating idea just yet. There were downsides to everything in life. Sylvia didn't want the liars, cheats and lowlifes to ruin it for her. There had to be a decent man out there somewhere. Afterall, if Sylvia was using a dating site, then it stood to reason that a decent man might use a site as well. Sylvia decided to give it another month and see if her luck changed.

Tammy was pleased with the change in Sylvia. For the past week, Sylvia had had a smile on her face, and her mobile phone stuck to her hand like glue. There was a clear difference about her – others saw and mentioned it too – so it wasn't just Tammy who picked up on the new vibe. She was happier, walked with more confidence, and constantly smiled. The change was due to 2 men. Both from the dating site, and both wanted to meet Sylvia. After seeing the change in Sylvia, Tammy was willing to admit the online dating scene might not be all bad, but she still had her reservations.

Sylvia was talking about arranging dates with the men. What if they turned out to be fakes? What if they had been setting her up just for a laugh? Or worse, what if one of them turned out to be just like her ex? Kev was an arsehole; a wanker, and they were his good points.

Sylvia had fallen deeply in love with Kev, he was the first boyfriend Sylvia had ever introduced to her family and friends. Kev had used Sylvia, her love, good nature and took what he wanted when he wanted. He not only broke Sylvia's heart once, but repeatedly. He always flirted with other women, always had more than one girlfriend on the go, and had a knack for making Sylvia feel worthless and to blame at the same time. If that wasn't enough, he had the damn nerve to keep coming back.

Every time he was at a loose end, or feeling a bit down, he would go crawling back to Sylvia. She would forgive him and make him feel fantastic as she dropped everything in the hope it would work that time. It never did, he always left. Every time.

Tammy had been there each time. She had been a shoulder to cry on – there were always many tears – and a venting board.

Tammy had tried – always in vein – to get Sylvia to see Kev for the scum he truly was. Finally, Sylvia had done just that. She was moving on, leaving Kev behind and searching for better.

Tammy kept her fingers crossed and hoped Sylvia would get what she deserved and not another crushing blow.

Kev had been secretly speaking to Sylvia while using the profile name Romanticfool. Women were easy to manipulate; they thought a man could be romantic without wanting something in return. Kev found women responded better when he used usernames with the words romantic or honest in it. He had her hooked again – he could always tell – and soon they would meet up. Kev could see Sylvia walk in and find him there, realisation would hit that it was him she had been talking to all along, and she would see how they are meant to be. She would have to accept the truth, she belonged to him. Kev knew Sylvia so well; he was able to reply in ways he knew would get her interested. He knew what questions to ask, answers to give, how to steer the conversation to let her do most of the talking. Sylvia was a typical lonely woman, wanted to hear sweet, soppy bullshit, and was very eager to believe.

When Kev had first seen Sylvia's profile, he was slightly amused – Sylvia was nothing special to look at – but mostly he had been infuriated. Kev hadn't fully got rid of her yet and as such, she should be moping in the background, waiting for his return. Kev cheated on her every chance he got – and always would – but the thought of another man touching Sylvia drove him crazy.

Sometimes Sylvia was online but not talking to him, she must be speaking to someone else. If Kev ever found out who, he would kill the little worm. Kev knew he had her where he wanted her, but if there was no competition it would be easier. He would just have to push for a date sooner and get to her before the other guy. Kev didn't want Sylvia all to himself to be with her and treat her right, he wanted her pining after him, waiting for him and with nobody else in sight. He had her that way once, and he could do it again. That was how it should be.

Sylvia was smitten. In the past week, she had 2 men chatting to her. Her phone had been constantly beeping with notifications from them. Sylvia always walked around with a smile on her face and, if she was honest, she loved the excitement. The attention. It was very easy to get caught up in it all and to start to feel something for either or both men with the constant messaging, but Sylvia held back. She didn't want an online relationship. She wanted something real, someone she could touch, hold, kiss. Someone she could come home too, and know they had her back as she had theirs. Having 2 men after her felt great, but at the same time she also felt as if she was cheating, and that fact didn't sit well with her. Sylvia felt like she was being dishonest by chatting with 2 men at once. She had only spoken to both men online and was not technically in a relationship with either of them but, still felt like she was betraying them. They had met on a dating site so it was implied that more than one person could be interested and talking to others, but it just felt wrong somehow.

Sylvia was not made for online dating. Thankfully, there were 2 men who both liked and wanted to meet her. Sylvia hoped with everything in her that one of them would turn out to be Mr Right, and she could finally have a happy ending.

Romanticfool was easy to talk to, it was as if they had known each other for years. Sylvia really liked him, but he refused to show her a picture of himself which put Sylvia off. What was he hiding? He was confident – almost cocky sometimes – when he spoke, so why refuse to show himself? It was a red flag, as Tammy kept pointing out to her. In fairness to him, that was the only thing he had going against him. But it was a biggie and Sylvia couldn't put her finger on it, but something just seemed off. He seemed too good to be true. Maybe it was just because he hid away that put that thought in Sylvia's mind, but she couldn't shake it off.

Genguywilts was the other man she had been chatting too. Sylvia had already argued with him but instead of that putting her off, it made Sylvia like him more. It showed he was passionate about things and unlike her ex – who would sulk and belittler her if he were wrong or lost an argument – Genguywilts allowed her to have her say and then they both agreed to disagree and moved on from the topic. It had been very refreshing. He also had a picture of himself which helped. Sylvia could admit to herself that she leaned more towards him and just hoped he was the same way – looks and conversation – in person.

Next thing to sort out was the dates. Sylvia didn't need Tammy to tell her she needed to be safe and smart about it, that she needed to make sure it was in public, she had enough common sense to know that anyway. There was more to it than just that though. Sylvia used the buses, so wherever she picked would need to be in quick walking distance to a bus, that ran every few minutes – and not because she was lazy, but in case she needed to make a quick run for it – and get back safely. The place also needed to be somewhere that made her feel comfortable and at ease, also a place where Tammy could easily hide to keep and eye out for her, make sure her date didn't to slip anything in her drink, or worse. A place that served food so they could sit and chat and have a proper date.

As Sylvia had 2 men to make dates with, then Sylvia needed 2 places that matched all her requirements. She was not about to take both men to the same place. What if the first date went well but then Sylvia took her 2nd date to the same place and her earlier date was still there. No, that would not be good. Sylvia wanted 2 different places, but preferably just a simple bus ride between them. She needed Tammy's help. Sylvia picked up the phone and rang her.

Tammy was pleased Sylvia had rung. Tammy had been itching to find out how things had been going. She had asked Sylvia, but Sylvia didn't like to talk about it, she was a private woman. Sylvia also had a bad habit – in Tammy's opinion – of believing something would go wrong if she spoke about it too much. In fairness, that did usually tend to be the case, but it was more of Sylvia always looking for the bad to happen instead of some divine curse against her.

Tammy had seen and was pleased by the change in Sylvia since joining the online dating site, but she still had her reservations. They had both looked up many different chat groups where people spoke about their experiences with online dating. There were many happy ending stories, and sadly, some very dangerous warning stories. Some no starters as well which amused Tammy. Those stories consisted of there being a great spark online but once in person, there was nothing, as if they had never spoken before. Tammy didn't understand how that was possible, they had been speaking for ages – some even months before meeting in person – but then they had nothing to say to each other? How was that possible? Tammy hoped it didn't happen to Sylvia.

'That was good timing,' Sylvia finished stirring the cup of tea and handed it to Tammy as she walked in.

'Thanks, I try,' Tammy laughed as she walked into the living room, followed by Sylvia.

Sylvia had already started looking for places. She had printed off every restaurant, diner, and pub – that served food – within a 3-mile radius of her home and on a bus route. Or close by a bus route. Sylvia gave Tammy half the sheets and they began to give places ticks for every requirement they matched. Then they placed them into piles.

It didn't take long, as soon they had finished. They picked up the pile containing the most ticks – 3 pages in total – and looked through them again, together this time. 2 were in easy distance of each other – 3 bus stops away – so Sylvia and Tammy picked them as the places for her dates.

Sylvia checked her messages and made sure both men wanted to meet in person. Sylvia flipped a coin to see who she would meet first, and which place they would have their date.

Sylvia paced around the living room. One hour left before she met her first date and her nerves were getting the better of her. She felt like she was going on a blind date. Not strictly accurate as Sylvia had been speaking to her dates – daily – for weeks, but it was the first time in person, so felt like a blind date.

Genguywilts was her first date. Sylvia hadn't told either date she had a date planned for both of them on the same night, that would have been too much. Genguywilts had been very easy about the arrangements, he agreed to the place, date and time, and even suggested she bring a friend if that would make her feel more comfortable. Sylvia was bringing Tammy, but in secret.

Romanticfool on the other hand had twice tried to make Sylvia change the details for their date, but Sylvia had stuck to her guns. She was very proud of herself – it wasn't something she ever did – and he eventually agreed to her terms. It had put a dampener on their date, and it hadn't even happened yet. Sylvia put it down to excitement on his part and tried to forget about it.

'Will you stop it. Everything will go swimmingly, and I will be there to knock him out if he turns out to be a waste of space. Now, you got everything?'

Sylvia did her check list – phone, keys, cash, bus card and fags – then grabbed her coat and followed Tammy out the door. They got on and off the bus together, but Tammy held back when Sylvia turned the corner and let her walk the last bit by herself. Tammy counted to 10, crossed the road and stood opposite. She watched as Sylvia went in, met her date and they sat down. Tammy watched as they ordered drinks, then crossed the road and entered.

Brian was his real name and his profile picture didn't do him justice. They began speaking and it was only when Sylvia saw Tammy get up and leave, that she realised just how at ease she felt.

Tammy was pleased with what she had seen so far and felt comfortable leaving Sylvia for a while. Tammy had to admit the guy seemed genuine, and there was no mistaking the twinkle in his eyes when Sylvia spoke. If Tammy were a romantic, she would swear it had all the hallmarks of love at first sight. She took one last look toward the happy couple before she left, something had come to her attention a few days ago and she needed to sort it out. She would be back within the hour though to check on Sylvia.

Kev was on cloud 9. Sylvia would soon be all his again, he was sure of it. Ever since he got the message from her asking for them to meet in person, Kev knew she would be under his control once again. Kev could just imagine it, Sylvia sat waiting for him to show up, he walks in and Sylvia would know there was no escaping him. She would be confused to see him and maybe a little annoyed – he expected it – but it would soon pass once she realised she belonged to him, always had and always would.

He would give her some cock and bull about missing her and wanting her to fall in love with the real him all over again which is why he never showed her a picture of himself. He was good at thinking on his feet and knew she would be eating out of the palm of his hands before the night was over.

In his own special, territorial way, he did miss Sylvia. He missed knowing she was there in the background waiting for him. He missed her constant need to please him and try to keep him. He just wasn't made for one woman alone. He needed more. He wanted more. He would always go after more. He just wanted Sylvia back there waiting as well.

Kev checked himself in the mirror – damn he looked good – grabbed his coat from the hook and left. Kev intentionally got there a little late, he wanted Sylvia settled with a drink before she saw him as it would be easier that way, less chance of her just walking out. Kev sent a quick text full lies to his current bit of squeeze, took a deep breath and entered.

Sylvia wasn't there. Kev looked around – she should be close by so she could recognise the red rose on his shirt he said he would wear – but she was nowhere to be seen.

'Hello Kev,' Kev turned to see who called his name. He saw Tammy stood behind him, to his left.

'What the fuck are you doing here? Where's Sylvia?'

Tammy smiled and took a step closer.

'Sylvia is on a date with a real man. Now you listen to me, and you listen good. Leave Sylvia alone! She's done with you.'

'She loves me. She will always be mine. She gave me her

heart.'

'Yes, and you trampled all over it you piece of shit! She has finally seen just what a complete waste of space you really are and moved on. She doesn't love you anymore. She doesn't want anything to do with you ever again. Now get that through your thick fucking skull and stay out of her life!'

Tammy walked away. She enjoyed the look of anger and bewilderment mixed on Kev's face. She knew he wouldn't drop it just like that, Kev never liked being told what to do – especially by a woman – and he had to end it, not the other way around. But tough shit. Tammy would do whatever it took to keep him away from Sylvia, and anything she could to help Sylvia move on and be happy.

It was Kev's own fault he was outed. He just couldn't help himself. He had to give the perfect answers. Always saying the right thing. It made Tammy think something was very wrong. Kev was meant to be Sylvia's first date, but with her suspicions, Tammy had managed to get Sylvia to change them around.

It had given Tammy time to do what she needed to do and let Sylvia enjoy a lovely date without having to face Kev again.

Tammy stood outside and instantly spotted Sylvia. She was positively glowing, laughing and Tammy honestly couldn't remember the last time she had seen Sylvia so happy. Tammy changed her mind about internet dating. If it could bring Sylvia back out of her shell and smile again, then it couldn't be all that bad.

PETER VS SHELBY

Peter threw the empty can across the road. Direct hit. The can hit the elderly woman stood at the bus stop. She let out a cry and waved her fists at Peter and his friends. They laughed. Ron took a step forward – as if he were going to cross the road, to go to the bus stop – the elderly woman moved as deep into the bus stop as she could. Peter and his friends laughed louder.

Shelby needed to go to the shops. They were out of bread and milk, but he had no intention of going outside yet. Shelby could see Peter and his friends at the end of his road. If he tried to leave now, he would only get hassled, and still not get the bread and milk. Peter thought he was the bee's knee's, when really, he was just an arrogant bully.

Peter won the cross-country championship 3 years in a row, this allowed him to get away with things. Not done his homework, blame it on training and get a free ride. Same for most other things. People allowed him to get away with things and Peter just got worse and worse.

It was people like the elderly woman and Shelby who bore the brunt of Peter's arrogance. Peter had always been a little shit, but he had gotten so much worse over the last few years. Shelby was what was called big boned, he had always been a big lad. He had the stature of a shit brickhouse – even from a baby – but a heart of gold. People were wary of Shelby until they realised, he was a gentle giant.

Except Peter and his friends. They seemed to take great pleasure in tormenting him. Maybe because he was so big, they considered it a challenge. Or maybe they got a thrill out of trying to make someone so big cry. Whatever the reason, Shelby had had enough. He didn't want any trouble., he just wanted an easy life. Shelby only wanted to finish school, go to college and then university. He wasn't sure what he wanted for career, just that he wanted to get away and stay away.

'Shelby dear, are you going to the shops?' Shelby's mum called from upstairs.

Peter and his friends hadn't moved. They would most likely be there for the rest of the evening. It was their usual habit. For all Peter's abilities, he did nothing with them outside of the cross-country. Shelby wished he had move as fast as Peter. Shelby wished he were as popular as Peter. Shelby was liked, but not popular.

'I'm just leaving now mum,' there was nothing else he could do. Shelby had to go to the shop. He just wished they would get bored with him soon and Shelby would be able to get what he needed. With dread and dismay in every step, Shelby walked towards the shop.

He got to Peter and his friends and kept walking. The shouts and insults had already started before Shelby reached them. Shelby ignored them and carried on. He managed to make it to the shops and get the bread and milk. They were waiting outside for him. They stood blocking his way.

Shelby tried to push past, but Peter tripped him over. The milk bottle smashed, milk poured over the pavement. He needed that, there was no money to get anymore for a few days. He would be living off of cereal as it was but now it would be dry cereal. His home life was poor, and Peter was making every other aspect of his life unbearable. Shelby couldn't take much more. He would snap soon.

Shelby stood up. Took several deep breaths and tried to get past them again. He was doing all he could not to cry. Shelby would not give them the satisfaction.

Peter could see Shelby struggling. Peter was loving it. Peter got a buzz from making people feel small. There was no other explanation. He simply enjoyed it. His speed allowed him to get benefits others couldn't, and that made him feel superior. He was better than them. He was faster. He was a champion.

Peter despised Shelby. He was a lump of lard and poor. Peter detested both things. Peter knew Shelby was close to tears. If he kept pushing, he was sure he would finally see Shelby break. Peter tripped Shelby over again. Peter tried to push Shelby's face into the spilled milk. Shelby reached his breaking point. Shelby grabbed Peter's leg and flipped Peter over.

'Fuck off Peter. I've had enough. Now leave me alone. I won't tell you again.'

Who did he think he was! Peter was livid. How dare this lump talk to him like that. Everybody knew who Peter was, but only a few knew who Shelby was, yet he had the audacity to speak to him that way. It would not stand.

'Don't you fucking dare talk to me like that. Who the fuck do you think you are? You are nothing. Nobody. Worthless air stealer,' Peter smirked. His friends laughed.

'I'm the nothing who will break your fucking legs if you try to trip me again,' Shelby was finally defending himself. He was not going to back down. He was not going to take Peter's shit anymore.

Peter could not, and would not, let Shelby talk to him like that. He had to do something, anything, to show him who was boss. Peter took a swing at Shelby. Peter was faster, but Shelby was stronger. Shelby threw a punch at Peter, and Peter went straight down. Peter was out cold after just one punch. Peter's friends stood gobsmacked. They knew they should help Peter, but none of them wanted to go up against Shelby. Like all bullies, they were cowards at heart. Shelby had just shown he could look after himself.

Ron, and the rest of Peter's friends moved out of the way. They let Shelby pass. Shelby strolled past them – keeping his cool as best he could – but once he was out of their view, he ran the rest of the way home. Shelby was shitting himself. What had he done? Why had he let Peter push him like that? Shelby knew it wasn't the end. Peter was not going to let things lie. Shelby had knocked Peter out with one punch and Peter wouldn't be able to let that stand, he had a reputation to think about.

That was bad news for Shelby. Peter would want revenge. He would want to punish Shelby. Peter thought of himself as a hard man, as a winner. Not the type of person to get knocked out by one punch. Shelby had really done it now. He thought he had it hard before, things were going to get much worse. Shelby did not want any of it. He just wanted to live in peace and get on with his life.

Peter was furious. He wanted to go to Shelby's and set the place on fire. Shelby needed to be punished. He couldn't get away with it. Peter was better than him, Peter was faster than him. Peter was a champion. Shelby was nothing. Shelby was a lump of lard, but Shelby had beat Peter. That would not stand. Peter had to do something about it. He had to be on top again. Peter got the spare petrol can his mum kept for emergencies in her car and made his way towards Shelby's.

'Don't be stupid Pete. You can't do that,' Ron stood blocking his path.

'I can't let him get away with it Ron. I ain't a mug, and I won't be treated like one. He needs to pay,' Peter tried pushing past Ron, but more of their friends helped Ron keep Peter back.

'Too right he does mate, but not like this. Too many people saw what happened. If his place goes up in smoke, it will be obvious you did it.'

'So what? I put this town on the map. No fucker will arrest me.'

'You are probably right, but with suspicion hanging over you, they won't let you compete in the race.'

Peter hadn't thought about that. The race was what made him indestructible. If he couldn't race, he would lose respect. He would lose his free ride. Peter would have to let things lie for now. Let Shelby think he had got away with it, and then Peter would show him who was boss.

'Ok, but this ain't over. He will pay.'

Ron was relieved Peter had seen sense. Peter was his meal ticket. They had been friends since they could walk. Ron was always by Peter's side. Peter had become more of a prick the last few years, but Ron stuck with him because of the freebies Peter got. New trainers and clothes from sponsors. Free food from local cafes. Leeway at school, blamed on training. It was great. Ron got the spare clothes Peter didn't want. Ron got the free food and drinks when he was with Peter, and they bunked off school most days. Ron didn't want to see all that go. He loved his life. He needed Peter to stay on top. Shelby would pay, he would have too. Peter wouldn't let it go. But Shelby would have to pay a different way. They would think of something special just for him. It would be epic.

Shelby had been a nervous wreck for the first few days after he knocked Peter out, but nothing had happened. There was no comeback from Peter or his friends. They had steered clear of him, made a point of not being in the same room as him. Others began to avoid Shelby as well, they didn't want to get on the wrong side of Peter.

Shelby didn't mind. The old saying was true, you know who your friends were when it really mattered. All it meant was Shelby had more peace, which he enjoyed. Shelby loved his own company, so less people around did not bother him at all. When Peter realised Shelby was unaffected, he kicked things up a notch.

Still careful not to do anything stupid and get suspended from the race, Peter began a different tactic. Peter and his friends hung around outside Shelby's block of flats. Morning to night they sat on the carpark border wall. They drank. They talked loudly. They made unpleasant comments about Shelby. They began on his mum. They made rude remarks to her when she ventured outside. They banged on his door and ran away. It was Peter's friends who did it, Peter told them what to do but, didn't do any of it himself. He could not be blamed for what other people did; he was in the clear. It was obvious he was behind it though. When Shelby's mum became too scared to leave their flat, became withdrawn and a shell of her former self. Shelby hit breaking point. To bully him was one thing, but not his mum. Not his family.

Shelby went outside. He walked up to them all and in no uncertain terms, told them to fuck off. They laughed. Shelby had expected as much. Ron took out his phone and started recording. Peter was acting innocent, with a confused look on his face, he was pretending he had no clue why Shelby was shouting at him. it would look like Shelby was the bully.

Peter was loving it but hid it well. Shelby soon realised their game and knew he couldn't hit Peter – no matter how much he really wanted to – so came up with a new idea.

'You think you are the best thing to happen to this town Peter, but you're wrong. You could have been great, but you are too stupid to understand what you had, and what you wasted. So I have to teach you.'

'Oh, and how are you going to do that?' Peter found it difficult to hide his glee. Shelby couldn't do a damn thing and they both knew it.

'I am going to take your title away from you.'

'What the fuck you on about? You think you can beat me. In a race? You're off your fucking rocker!' Peter laughed so hard he fell off the wall. He laughed even harder.

'Just watch me,' Shelby walked off. They were all laughing now. Peter was faster than Shelby, but he was also very cocky. He was an arrogant little prick and Shelby would use that against him. Shelby knew he couldn't beat Peter in a straight race, but he could distract him enough to let someone else win. Peter would still lose his title, as Shelby promised.

3 weeks before the race. Shelby spent them training. He needed to be faster, to make Peter think he was serious. Shelby made sure he ran in front or Peter and his friends. He wanted them to see him, to take him seriously. While it was unlikely, they would feel threatened, others would be encouraged. Word soon spread about the challenge. Peter himself had told many people –

in the hopes of dismaying Shelby from competing – but it had the opposite reaction. Instead of mocking Shelby – although many did when Peter was present – they encouraged Shelby to win. Everyone wanted to see what would happen. Everyone wanted to see how well Shelby would do. Shelby could never win a race – it was too late to officially enter – but he was allowed to run alongside the racers and that would be an advantage. Shelby didn't have the pressure from the race, he only needed to make sure Peter lost.

The day of the race arrived, and Shelby got there early. He wanted to set Peter on edge as quickly as possible. The sooner he got on his nerves, the better.

Peter saw Shelby waiting. He would enjoy beating him, Shelby would never disrespect him again. He would be firmly put in his place. As a bonus, others would think twice about messing with him as well. Some had already started to think they could disrespect him thanks to Shelby. It would be fun, Peter was looking forward to it.

The racers took their starting positions. Peter and Shelby could see each other, Peter tried staring Shelby out, but Shelby just turned away. The more he could rile him up, the better. The whistle blew and the race started. Peter took the lead, followed closely by 3 others. Shelby was towards the end, but not the last. Peter looked back and saw Shelby slowly making progress. Peter was far in front but, he hadn't expected Shelby to do so well. Peter had expected Shelby to be further behind. Peter Ran faster, he wanted to leave a clear gap between them, to show who was boss.

Shelby made slow progress. He didn't want to use up all his energy at the start. He wanted to scare Peter a little later and would need his energy. People cheered for Shelby. It annoyed Peter, few were cheering for him. He would need to deal with that once the race was over.

The race turned a bend, and Shelby was lost from sight. Shelby cut out of the race. He took a left instead of a right and took a short cut. He had lived in the town all his life, he knew the roads intimately. Like everyone else, he had watched the race many times over the years and knew the course. He wasn't officially in the race so he couldn't win, and it wasn't technically cheating. Shelby jumped on his bike – he had placed on the corner before the race – and rode towards the last bend in the race. Shelby hid his bike and re-joined the race.

Peter was still ahead. He had a young lad on his tail, and he was panting hard. He hadn't trained as much as he should have.

Shelby ran as hard and as fast as he could. He shouted out for Peter, called his name again and again, as loud as he could. Peter turned to see who was shouting at him and couldn't believe his eyes. It had to be a trick. There was no way Shelby could be that close to him. Peter watched as Shelby gained on him. Peter ran with everything he had left. Peter ran and ran, but Shelby stayed close behind.

When Peter looked back again, Shelby was gone. Caught up in the moment, Peter forgot what he was doing and stopped running. The shock made him stand still, and look around, trying to find Shelby.

The young lad ran past Peter, but Peter didn't notice. He was still looking for Shelby. He was gone.

Then he was back again. Shelby came out from behind 2 other racers and darted past Peter. He couldn't believe it. It took a few seconds to register what had happened, and for his feet to start moving again, but it was too late.

The young lad crossed the finish line, and Shelby beat him. By the time Peter crossed the finish line, he was in 8th place. It was his worst lose ever. He had lost the race and been beat by Shelby.

Peter couldn't stand it. With the last of his energy, he ran up to Shelby who was being congratulated by so many people.

Seeing red Peter yelled at Shelby.

'You cheating bastard! There was no way you beat me fairly.'

'Who said anything about beating you fairly? The challenge was I would make you lose. Take your title away, and that's what I did.'

DAY TRIP

The coach pulled in at the station. Everyone took their time getting off but, eventually Mrs James made it off the coach. She felt the cool, slightly breeze against her face and smiled. If she finished her job early, she would take a stroll along the beach. She hadn't done anything like that in years. The weather was good, dry, and breezy to combat the heat.

Mrs James made her way out of the bus station and stood aside to allow the other people to get past. She needed to get her bearings before she could start.

'Doris dear, are you coming to the beach with us?'

'Not just yet Mavis. I have something I need to do first. I will join you there later,' Mavis wasn't happy, but left with a group of others, leaving Mrs James to her own devices. Mrs James disliked Mavis at the best of times, and today she needed to be alone to do her work. She didn't need – or want – and audience.

Secretly, Mrs James hoped one day she would get the call for Mavis – she could annoy the saintliest of people – she would even contemplate doing it for free. In the meantime, there was work to be done.

It had been several years since Mrs James had last been to Weymouth. She remembered the summer day trips she used to take with her parents and little brother. Her mum sat on the beach reading the latest Mills & Boons book, while her dad went to the pub. Her brother and herself would try to see how close to the sea they could get before they got stuck in the mud. The memory brought a smile to her face.

People were looking at her, it didn't matter. Those days were long gone, and Mrs James enjoyed the attention. Just not while she was working.

The town had changed so much in the years since she had last been there. Mrs James was unsure which way she needed to go. She didn't want to ask for directions – that sort of thing might be remembered and cause her no end of trouble – and she couldn't work out how to use the google map function on her mobile. There was only one thing for it, time to go shopping.

Mrs James headed in the direction of the Highstreet – every town had a Highstreet, or something close to one – found a shop that sold maps and purchased one for the local area. Mrs James went back out of the shop, walked a little further up the path and found a bench to sit on. Mrs James opened the map. She took out a piece of paper she had wrote the name and address on and checked it on the map. She spotted the road easily enough.

Mrs James asked a passer by what road she was on and checked it on the map. According to the map, the street she needed would be a left at the end of the road she was on, then right at the end of that road, and then second left. It looked simple enough.

Mrs James checked her watch. She had over 4 more hours before she needed to be back on the coach to go back home. Plenty of time to complete her job and enjoy a walk on the beach.

Mrs James made it to her destination in less than 20 minutes. She was very pleased with herself. Those exercises Maggie was making her do every morning were not a waste of time after all. Mrs James made a mental note to thank Maggie when she next saw her.

There was no visible doorbell, so Mrs James tapped her knuckles against the glass stained window, a rose. After only a few a few seconds Mrs James could see a shadow. It got bigger as someone moved closer to the door. The door opened partially, and a woman's face peered through the gap.

Mary wasn't expecting anyone. She didn't know the woman standing at the door, but she seemed harmless enough.

Mary opened the door and stood facing her visitor.

'Hello?'

'So sorry to trouble you dear, I was wondering if you would be so kind and let me have a glass of water? The heat is too much.'

Mrs James was hunched up, to add credence to what she said. She looked hot and in discomfort.

'Of course, please come in and sit-down a while,' Mary would not usually let complete strangers into the house, but the woman looked in pain, and Mary couldn't bare to leave her to suffer. She felt no fear, or apprehension.

'Thank you so much, it's very kind of you.'

Mary led Mrs James through to the living room. It was spacious and well decorated. Mrs James hopes she wouldn't make too much of a mess when she did her job. It would be a shame to ruin it.

Mrs James sat down on the sofa, while Mary fetched her a drink. Mary came back with a glass of water and sat next to Mrs James on the sofa. They made small talk for a while and when Mrs James got bored, she pulled the knife out and swiped at Mary.

Mary fell to the ground, confused and in pain. It was unexpected. Mary had no way of defending herself. The knife came at her once more, this time there was nowhere Mary could move.

The knife came down hard and fast. It was a clean cut. It was over in a matter of seconds. Some blood sprayed on the walls, and a small pool of blood on the white carpet.

Mrs James bent over and closed Mary's eyes. Open eyes of her victims never bothered Mrs James, but it had been requested. So, she did it.

Mrs James kept looking at the carpet, the blood would stain if someone didn't clean it up soon. That would not happen though. Mrs James was not about to clean – even if she hated stains – and Mary's family were not due back until the next day.

A very small part of Mrs James felt sadness that Mary had died. She seemed a pleasant woman. She seemed kind and caring. But a paying job was a paying job. Money was work, so work needed to be done. Living did not come cheaply.

Mrs James wiped the knife on the carpet – it was ruined anyway – and put it back in her handbag. Mrs James picked up her glass of water and went to the kitchen, she emptied the remaining water in the sink and put the glass in her handbag. She had touched nothing else. Mrs James went back into the living room for one last look at the scene. She wanted to make absolutely sure she hadn't missed anything. Too many people did the deed then got away from the scene as quickly as possible and left something unwanted behind. Mrs James preferred to stay for a few more minutes and make sure she had removed every trace of anything that could lead back to her. That was why she was still in the business, all these years later. Mrs James was known for her efficiency, on the job, and afterwards.

Mrs James checked her watch again. They had been making small talk for longer than Mrs James had thought. She now had a little under 3 hours left before she needed to get back on the coach and go home.

Mrs James went into the hallway and rooted around in her bag. She took out a little knitted doll – hand made by herself – with Mary stitched on the chest and placed it on the welcome mat. It was her signature move. For years Mrs James never bothered with anything as egotistic as a signature, but then she got fed up with other people taking credit for her work. The doll had been an accident as a signature.

Mrs James made a doll for each job and kept it in her handbag until the job was done, then kept it as a souvenir. After a job, many years ago, it had fallen mistakenly out of her handbag while she was outing her knife away. Mrs James had heard a noise and been startled. A gate opening sound had panicked Mrs James and she never noticed she had dropped the doll. It wasn't until later, when the police found it, and it was plashed all over the papers that Mrs James realised her error.

It had been her one mistake, but she used it to her advantage. The people who hired her had assumed it was her signature and she went along with it. Mrs James made dolls for all her jobs and took them with her from then on. Mrs James still made a doll as a souvenir, but she also made one for the crime scene.

It was time to leave. There was nothing left for Mrs James to do. She quietly went back out the front door and casually walked away. Mrs James made her way back to the Highstreet and to a local café. She was always hungry after she completed a job for some reason. Mrs James ordered an all-day breakfast. She took her time, enjoying the noises around her. When she finished, Mrs James headed towards the beach. It was still a lovely day, and Mrs James intended to enjoy the beach before she left for home.

Mrs James was on the coach headed back home. It had just pulled up outside the retirement home. Mrs James waited for her friends to get off the coach first. Mrs James made a big deal about needing help to get off the coach.

'It's been such a long day; I think I my joints have seized up a bit dear.'

'Not to worry Doris. I will have you back in your room in no time,' Jade, a care assistant at the home, helped Mrs James into a wheelchair. Jade pushed Mrs James to her room and helped her onto her bed.

'Tea will be served shortly. Would you like me to bring you some?'

'Yes please dear, that would be lovely.'

Jade shut Mrs James's bedroom door and walked off to help others. Mrs James waited a few seconds, she heard no movements outside. Mrs James got up and went over to her wardrobe. At the bottom – under her old pyjamas, she never wore – was her souvenir box. Mrs James lifted it out and placed it on her bed. She opened it up and took out the second doll from her handbag, Mrs James gave the doll a kiss then placed it with the others in the box. Mrs James closed the box, put it back in her wardrobe, and got back onto her bed.

A few minutes later Jade knocked on her door. She had Mrs James's cup of tea.

'Did you have a good day at the beach Mrs James?'

'Oh yes dear, everything went perfectly. I couldn't have planned it better if I tried.'

I WON'T QUIT

Gary couldn't believe what he was hearing. It had to be illegal surely. How could it not be? It was his life, his choice. Why was it ok to be forced into something else?

'You can't withhold my meds. You're my doctor, you know I need my insulin.'

'I'm sorry Gary, but it's a new government initiative to help people quit smoking. It's for your own good. You must attend the meeting. I can not prescribe your medication until I have been told you have attended. My hands are tied,' Dr Welder hated the new initiative as much as his patients did.

He was deemed the bad guy and had to bear the brunt of his patients dismay and anger. He understood the reason behind the initiative, it was good. People shouldn't be smoking full stop, but those with health issues – especially breathing problems – like Gary, really shouldn't be smoking at all. They were making it harder for themselves and costing the NHS money that could be used for better things. To help people who were not actively killing themselves. Dr Welder agreed with the initiative in principle but wished there were a better way to implement it. So he wouldn't have to deal with situations like this.

'Ok, so say I go to the meeting. Do I have to participate?'

'No, you just have to attend and stay until the end of the meeting.'

'How many meetings do I have to go too?'

'Just the one. At the moment, the initiative is one meeting a year for those on repeat prescriptions.'

Dr Welder handed Gary a leaflet which outlined the initiative and gave a number he needed to ring to arrange a meeting he could attend.

Gary was furious. He wasn't killing anyone. Druggies could get medication for free, daily, but he was being refused because he smoked. Prisoners could still get treatment, but now he was being refused because he smoked.

The country was meant to be great, but big brother was getting out of control. Gary bet those in charge didn't have to attend any stupid meeting to get their medications. Gary took the leaflet and left.

He only had 3 more days of insulin left, so if he couldn't get a meeting soon, he would be fucked. Nobody mentioned anything like this before, there had been no letter telling patients – or people in general – that this was a new thing. What if Gary needed heart medication or something as serious and was refused medication.

Nobody would care. It wasn't right. It wasn't fair. Gary did not have a choice, he couldn't just get his meds from over the counter, they had to be prescribed. There was nothing he could do except ring the number on the leaflet. He wasn't happy about it though.

The number was answered by a robotic woman's voice. Pick a number and wait on hold for ages. Gary was sure those in charge got kicks out of doing this type of thing to people. It wasn't a free number – never was when it was a forced number – and they didn't even play half decent hold music.

Almost 50 minutes Gary was on hold before someone spoke. He was asked his town, then given 3 options of places and times. He picked the one for later that day and gave his name. Gary was told to arrive early to make sure he could check in in plenty of time or he would have to go to another meeting if he missed the registration. The line went dead, the call was over. Rude prick, Gary thought as he checked his watch. The meeting was in 2 hours. He would need to get 2 buses to get there, and one ran every 30 minutes, but on the bright side there was a pub close by the meeting. Gary set off.

He got there with just over 40 minutes to spare, and decided to grab a quick bite to eat at the pub. It was quiet in the pub. The smoking ban had done many businesses harm, and now they had this new initiative. They damn well smoked themselves, the self-righteous hypocrites. Gary felt anger build in him and took deep breathes to calm himself down. He didn't want to be riled up when he went to the meeting. It wouldn't surprise him one bit if they were just aching to find a reason they could use to kick people out of the meeting so they would have to attend more meetings. Passive aggression at its best, the governments speciality.

The food was lovely, and Gary thought he must go back there sometime. He got up and left. The meeting was being held in the hall across the road. The traffic was light, and Gary made it to the hall without stopping. He was 15 minutes early and there were 4 others waiting already. The doors were locked, but lights were on inside and sounds of chairs being arranged could be heard inside.

Gary nodded at those already waiting, and 2 nodded back. The other 2 looked as if they could break the door down at any moment. After a few more minutes, the door were opened from the inside. A lady with a clipboard instructed everyone to form a queue and wait until they were called.

One by one they went in, gave their name, and were told to sit in the hall. It was a local community hall with children's pictures over the walls. Tables and more chairs were stacked together across one wall, and toilet signs could be seen by a door at the other end of the hall.

8 people showed up for the meeting. They were all sat and waiting for the person who would run it to show up. 10 minutes later, a middle-aged man showed up. He looked like he had ran to the hall and was flushed in the face. The chairs had been arranged in a circle. 2 were empty, one for a patient who hadn't shown up yet and the other for him. The man sat down, took out some

leaflets and a book from his briefcase, then introduced himself.

'Hello everyone, my name is Daniel. That you all for attending. We are here to discuss the harmfulness of smoking, to you and to others. First, I would like everyone to look at these,' he handed out the leaflets to everyone before continuing, 'I think you will find them very interesting.

The leaflet was one sheet, with information on both sides. It comprised of lists. What smoking was costing the NHS. The dangers of smoking and the benefits of quitting. It was nothing new as far as Gary was concerned. He folded it up and put it away in his pocket. He wasn't the only one who put it away without reading the nonsense on it.

In fact there was only one person who was reading it, and he was smiling as he read it. The man was in his 60's, he wore dishevelled clothes and looked like a nice chap.

Daniel noticed the man smiling and knew he was not going to get through to anyone there. It was going to be a long, wasted afternoon. He knew better than anyone that a person can not be forced to quit smoking. But nobody listened, and he had bills to pay, so he spoke at the meetings.

'Has everyone read the leaflet?' Daniel asked.

Some nodded, and others mumbled yes.

'Good. Now we are going to talk about a few of the dangers with smoking,' Daniel looked around the room.

3 people were looking at him, the others were either looking at the floor, or around the room and deliberately avoiding eye contact with him. He had a job to do so continued.

'84% of lung cancer is caused by smoking.'

'Can you prove that?' It was the smiling man who asked. He was staring at Daniel. Not aggressively or with malice, but with a look that said he wasn't going to be fobbed off.

'You have the information right in front of you sir. The numbers don't lie.'

'You haven't answered my question. Can you prove without a shadow of a doubt that those people would not have died from lung cancer if they never smoked?'

'As I have said sir, the numbers clearly show the answer. Those people died unnecessarily. If they did not smoke, they would not have died from lung disease.'

'Wait a minute, you say 84% were due to smoking. So, that means the other 16% had nothing to do with smoking. Which means smoking is not the only reason someone can get lung disease, and I am willing to bet my wages that a good majority, if not all, of those blamed on smoking actually had nothing to do with it. My point, is you can not go back in time and stop someone from smoking to see if they would have died from lung disease, or any other illness for that matter if they never smoked.'

'Well with all due respect sir, that is a copout. A way to deny facts and keep from hearing the ugly truth. Almost all smokers use an excuse like that. It is killing you, and others around you. That is a fact.'

'So does pollution from vehicles, but I don't see any drivers having to attend meetings on the dangers of pollution, so they can get petrol, or their insurance renewed. Rockets create holes in our atmosphere which is having damaging effects, but no space agency has to attend meetings on the dangers. Both of these examples – and I could give many more – are far worse than a smoker, yet we have been made to feel like we alone are killing the human race. Excuse my language, but that's bullshit. It is my body. You and nobody else, can tell me what I can and can not do with my own body.'

Daniel had a list of subjects he had to talk through before the meeting could be over. This was not one of the subjects, and Daniel wanted to put an end to it so they could get on with the meeting.

'Very well sir. You say I can not prove a person would not have been ill had they never smoked, and I say you can not prove smoking has ever saved anyone. At least with vehicles, they can help save lives by getting a person to medical assistance sooner. Rockets can educate us about space, and given time, I am sure we will be able to travel across the stars, which would not be possible without rockets. There is, however, no upside to smoking.'

That is where you are wrong. Smoking saved my life. Twice!' He was smiling again.

'Impossible!'

'Now who is hiding away from the facts? It is true and very possible as it happened. To me.'

There wasn't much Daniel could say. He couldn't outright call the man a liar – which he had to be – as Daniel didn't know if the man had a violent streak or not. Daniel saw the way the others were looking at the man, he could not kick him out as someone else might become violent, but he had to end it. He had to stop the man glorifying smoking. It was not a good thing, and it should never be praised.

'How did smoking save your life? Smoking kills, not the other way around.'

'I will tell you,' the man moved in his chair, making himself more comfortable before continuing, 'when I was growing up, smoking was everywhere. Smoking was allowed in hospitals, on buses, in restaurants etc, and there was none of the crap that goes with it today. people were free to smoke if they wanted too, and not be made to feel like a pariah. I remember visiting my aunt's house and the ceiling would be a grey cloud of smoke, and it didn't bother anyone. My aunt's house was always busy with people dropping by for a chat or a game of cards. Anyway, I started smoking for the same reason many people start – at least in my time – because someone else in the family smoked and it was just natural to do what they did when you thought they were amazing. Now before you start,' the man looked at Daniel, 'my mum didn't smoke, and it was my choice to smoke. I was always told growing up to never let anyone force me into doing anything I didn't want to do, and to be my own man, not just follow the crowd. That being said, yes, I did start smoking because my older brother smoked, and I thought he was the best. I don't regret my decision though, and never have. Life was good. Then when I was in my 30's, they banned smoking on buses and shortly after that was when smoking saved my life for the first time. I was a bus driver at the time, driving coaches. I don't remember the exact day, but I know it was a Tuesday afternoon towards the end of August. The coach was empty, and I was on my back to Swindon bus station, it was the end of my shift. The coach was getting over heated – the coach was old and needed replacing, but management wouldn't hear of it – it still worked so could still be used. I was early and wanted a smoke, so I parked up in a layby. I was supposed to stay on the coach at all times, but I could no longer smoke on it, so I got off. I stood away from the coach and as I sparked up, the engine blew. It burst into flames. I could see the smoke filling the little compartment I should have been sat in, and saw flames lick the seat. I wouldn't have stood a chance. It is only because I smoked and got out of the coach to have a smoke, that I lived. Smoking saved my life.'

The hall erupted in clapping. A few even shouted out of glee. Daniel knew he had no chance of getting even one of them to quit smoking. It was a losing battle, and he was on the wrong side. There was more he had to get through before the meeting was over, but he knew there was no point. Nobody would listen to him, and after that story he couldn't blame them.

They were swapping stories; he could hear them asking about the other time smoking saved the smiling man's life. Daniel got up and walked out. The job was a waste of time anyway, and he wasn't going to waste more of his afternoon when he had more chance of convincing a wall to move than he did with getting any of them to quit smoking. He had had enough of them.

It was a while before anyone noticed Daniel had left. They sat around for just a few more minutes, calling out his name, then they left. Gary went out with the others, most them headed towards the pub, with smiling man leading the way. His name was Jack, and Gary loved his story.

They stood outside the pub, light up their fags, and were glad the stupid meeting was over. They could get back on with their lives.

Printed in Poland
by Amazon Fulfillment
Poland Sp. z o.o., Wrocław